CLEMENTINE
SWITCHBOARD SISTERHOOD
JUNE MARIE SAXTON

ACKNOWLEDGEMENTS

"Appreciation is a wonderful thing: it makes what is excellent in others belong to us as well."

Voltaire

Special thanks to Shannyn S. Davis of Rust+Wire Photography for the cover design and layout of my book. Thanks to Allie Keetch for keeping the roar in the Roaring Twenties and bringing Clementine to life. My appreciation to the other authors writing in the Switchboard Sisterhood series.

Thanks to Casey Saxton for helping me with my newsletter and author website, and to Kynleigh Marie Davis for reading the story back to me, and with such gusto! I am grateful for my editor, Tristi Pinkston, and for those who read my work and encourage me graciously.

DEDICATED TO

The awkward girl I used to be—who made me hope for more.

And to the woman I yet will become—thanks for settling the score!

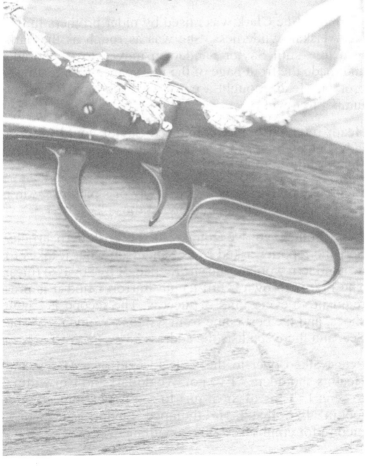

CHAPTER ONE

"A girl should be two things: classy and fabulous."

Coco Chanel

Clementine Clark was raised by older brothers in the Alaskan wilderness. She was as rough as the bark of a tree until Saylor Sanderson moved to Anchorage and made the front page of the newspaper. Clementine's brother, Heath, bought a copy when he took a load of lumber to town.

Heath returned home, convinced Saylor could make a lady out of his sister. "Read what it says right here," Heath said.

Heath's twin, Hardy, whistled at Saylor's picture. "Ain't no making Clementine into one of those."

"No, brother, you've gotta read the gosh-dern article. See, the reporter asked Miss Sanderson what it takes to be a modern woman, and she replied, 'I live by two rules. The first is to own a full-length mirror. I find it is pre-requisite to every kind of success. The second is...new shoes, and the best come from Ashtons Women's Shop.' See, and there she lists the address."

Pete walked over to the table to read over Hardy and Heath's shoulders. "I've got five dollars and I'm willing to send Li'l Sis to town just to see if she comes home lookin' like that." He thumped Saylor Sanderson's picture for emphasis. "Who's with me?"

Hardy reached for his wallet. "I'll put up five. Poor Clementine's grown up all bugs and sunshine. It was good enough for her when she was a little gal, but she's matured, and a feller wouldn't know her from a shrub! Just cuz we're bachelors don't mean Li'l Sis has gotta be one."

"I'm in," Heath said, pleased his brothers agreed with him. They hadn't the foggiest idea how to help Clementine be first, a girl, and second, a lady. "Let's face it, boys. We don't know beans about petticoats or pantaloons, bloomers or brassieres, or whatever else it was that set Ma apart from Pa. Ma would be disappointed in the way we've just let Sis run wild."

"Whatever she knows about bein' female, she's had to figure out from the hens and Hilde," Hardy said.

"Hilde's a mule. Now, Flossy and Blossom are better examples of womanhood all the way around, but there ain't no milk cows anywhere that knows about full-length mirrors and new shoes." Heath pulled another five-dollar bill from his billfold. "I'm payin' Matthew's share, since he ain't here right now."

And that's how it all began. Clementine Clark, also known as "Li'l Sis," rode into town on Hilde the mule. She wore her finest hand-me-down plaid flannel shirt and a clean pair of patched overalls. She had twenty dollars in her pocket and her brothers' instructions rolling through her head. She was supposed to buy a full-length mirror at Archer Merchandise, on credit, and then shop the sale racks at Ashton's Women's Shop.

"We ain't never done nothin' like this before," she said to the mule.

Hilde twitched one ear in response.

"I'm embarrassed to walk into that women's shop. I hope

that Miss Saylor's there so I don't have to explain the newspaper article. I just wanna be able to walk in and say, 'My brothers sent me to look like this, but I've only got twenty bucks,' because that's how Pete coached me."

That time, Hilde never said a thing because even a mule could see there wasn't enough money to fix all that was wrong with Clementine. Hilde parked herself in front of Ashton's Women's Shop. There was no need to tie her reins to the hitching post, but Clementine did it because it seemed responsible. "Well, here goes nothin'," she said, taking a deep breath.

The store smelled expensive—like leather and fine fabrics. Dresses of silks, satins, and chiffons hung neatly on racks. Clementine remembered very little of her mother, but she pictured her in pretty skirts and blouses like these.

A well-kept salesclerk looked at the out-of-towner as kindly as she possibly could. "Welcome to Ashton's. May I help you?"

"I've come to buy some shoes," Clementine announced.

"Shoes," the clerk repeated. The woman couldn't take her eyes off Clementine's plaid shirt—or maybe it was her wool cap that was so distracting. Clementine pulled it off her head, and a pile of long blonde hair fell like a waterfall. The action worked, as now the saleslady looked in the customer's eyes for the first time. "Of course. What do you have in mind?"

"I'm embarrassed to say I'd like something like that," Clementine said, pointing to a display of pretty high heels.

"Do you know what size you are?" the woman asked, trying hard not to judge.

"Not with these old woolies," Clementine said, pulling off a heavy boot. "But I believe I'm about three sizes smaller than Pete."

The woman arched a worried brow. "Pete?"

"These used to be his boots. I have to wear at least two pair of heavy socks to keep them from slippin' on my heels. They rub a gosh-dern blister faster than I can finish my chores if I don't sock up proper."

"I'm happy to measure you, but you can't wear two pairs of thick socks with dress shoes. Are you prepared to purchase silk stockings?"

"If I need to, I need to," Clementine declared.

Just then, the door opened, and a dainty bell chimed. The clerk looked up and Clementine wrenched around so she could see who'd come into the store. To Clementine's utter delight, it was that attractive gal from the *Anchorage Times*. Clementine called, "You're from the paper! I came to town today just to buy a mirror and new shoes. I bought the last mirror they had across the street."

Saylor Sanderson was precisely the kind of thoughtful woman who wouldn't refuse help to anyone. Clementine could see kindness in her eyes, so she took a deep breath and soldiered on. "I was raised by older brothers, so I don't know refinement or fashion, but the boys gave me five dollars apiece and sent me to town to follow your advice."

Miss Sanderson flashed a smile with the energy of her whole soul. Whenever Heath smiled like that, a tree was about to topple, and so Clementine Clark took heart. Today was the day things were happening in her life— the gosh-dern magical and necessary things that would make her fit for society. "You can't go wrong shopping here," the famous flapper replied. Miss Sanderson tossed an apologetic look at the gentleman she was with before putting an arm around Clementine, leading her toward a dressing room.

"If I can help further, I'll be over here," the perplexed saleslady said. It was clear Clementine Clark was Saylor's customer now. The doting gentleman echoed the words and walked behind the counter as well.

"Is that your man?" Clementine asked Saylor when they were out of earshot.

"I'm a modern, so I don't need a man, but I'll let you in on a secret. Miss Clark, I can't live without him," came Saylor's earnest reply. The words were so genuinely spoken that Clementine took note. She hoped to say such a thing one day!

"I only have twenty dollars—where should I start?"

"Do you have a job?"

"Not in town, but I'd like to find something," Clementine replied.

"What do you do now?" Saylor asked, pulling a couple of dresses off the rack. She was already fluttering over Clementine's situation, and they'd only just met. Clementine was feeling very pleased, being both seen *and* listened to.

"I stack and haul wood."

Saylor didn't grimace. She just went right on as if she met wood-hauling women in men's clodhoppers on a daily basis. "What would you *like* to do?" Saylor asked, already leading Clementine to the dressing room. "I know that Mr. Jason Tremblay at the Spruce Telephone Company is always looking for operators. I have a small connection if we need to use it."

Well, shucks! A switchboard operator? Clementine's heart leaped in her chest. Here was a modern woman believing Clementine could become what her brothers hoped she'd become—a genuine, honest-to-goodness, definable female with an income! "Who'd a thunk it?" Clementine asked incredulously.

Meanwhile, between bits of personal conversation, Saylor was teaching Clementine the basics. "If you have a nice, neutral-colored dress, you can coordinate it with different colors of cardigans, scarves, beads, hats, and shoes—Miss Clark, you can get a lot of milage out of a dress like this."

Clementine focused on the dress. It was the most beautiful garment she'd ever seen, and it sounded magical to pair it with so many things. Saylor showed her a variety of looks right while that dress hung on a fancy hook in the dressing room. "I only have twenty dollars," Clementine restated.

"Well, no matter what amount your brothers sent you to town with, I shall match it," Saylor said, completely undeterred.

"You must be an angel. Did my mother send you to help me?"

Saylor blinked back tears at the humble question, saying only, "Perhaps. Now, you just let me coordinate you and don't look at the tags. This is fun!"

"My brothers wouldn't want me to burden you like a charity case."

"Raspberries! Charity for who? I've always wanted to coordinate somebody. You are fulfilling my needs right now. I recommend you get the navy dress and the gray one." Saylor hesitated before adding, "And at least one fun plaid number."

"You were wearing plaid in the newspaper," Clementine said. "I've never owned more than two dresses at the same time in my whole life, and ever since I grew bosoms, I ain't had any."

Once the actual trying-on began, Saylor poked her head out of the dressing room, informing the clerk that underthings were necessary. Clementine hadn't owned a brassiere ever since she needed one. "My brothers were too embarrassed. Heath just recommended I tie a dishtowel around myself when needed. You know—to keep things from floppin' around."

"Yes," Saylor said, dismissing the gush of information as rapidly as it was received.

Once the heavy flannels and woolens were gone and the silky underthings went on, Clementine gasped to see her reflection. "I'm kind of purty," she admitted. "I never knew I was shaped quite like this. I mean, it's good, ain't it?"

Saylor smiled at her in the glass, knowing just how sound her advice had been. Success *did* hinge on a full-length mirror. Here was a tragic woman who didn't even know she was shapely and beautiful! "I am stepping out so I can properly marvel when you come out of the dressing room in a new ensemble." Of course, Saylor had to explain what an ensemble was. "That means a put-together outfit."

"I'm not sure she has money for all this," the clerk called from her perch behind the counter.

Clementine smiled to hear Saylor reply, "Oh, she does."

"You're not just purty on the outside, Miss Sanderson. You've got purty insides, too," Clementine called through the dressing room door.

Wearing a drop-waist navy chiffon dress and a red cloche hat, Clementine looked and felt like a modern woman, all right! She was no longer "Li'l Sis" because she felt sophisticated enough to smoke and wear lipstick. She said as much, and Saylor said, "You are a feminine flapper now, Clementine, but don't you dare smoke! It'll make your new clothes stink, not to mention all that pretty hair."

Saylor's beau came out of the stockroom with a stack of shoes. One by one, the pumps slid comfortably on her silk-stocking-clad feet. "Feels much better than Pete's old woolies and boots," Clementine remarked. She walked to a mirror, turning her feet this way and that, pleased to see how trendy she looked and felt.

For her original twenty bucks, and Saylor Sanderson's contributions, Clementine got three dresses, three pairs of shoes in navy, gray, and red, several scarves, necklaces, cardigans, hats, and two sets of delicate underthings, including the silk stockings. Once the items were wrapped in tissue paper, put in boxes, and tied with strings, Clementine said, "I don't know how to ride Hilde in my dress and balance all these packages."

"Andy delivers!" Saylor suggested brightly. The saleswoman clucked like a hen with a shell stuck in her gullet.

"Whatever Hilde is, I'm sure we can tie her on behind," Saylor continued, giving the greatest customer service experience of Clementine's lifetime.

"Hilde's a mule," Clementine offered.

"That's going to be a slow drive," Andy said.

Saylor pulled Andy away a few steps and whispered in his ear. He smiled something wonderful, and Saylor suggested Clementine follow her out to Andy's car with her packages.

"We haven't been formally introduced," the impeccably dressed saleswoman said, "but I'm Mrs. Ivy Ashton."

Saylor's eyes seemed to bug out of her head, but she handled the situation beautifully by saying, "Surely you are much too young to be Andy's mother."

Clementine observed the exchange, finding Saylor to be as socially magnificent as she was kind and lovely. She also realized Saylor didn't work at the store at all, and yet she'd successfully taken over the place like a well-mannered pirate. That wasn't what ruffled Mrs. Ashton, however, but the way Saylor had also commandeered her son.

Clementine rode in the rumble seat, leading Hilde out of town and conversing with her like a friend. "I feel like such a female now, Hilde. You can't imagine how liberatin' it is to show my legs and ankles. And my shoes! Look at my *lovely* new shoes. They call this color dove gray. Ain't that purty?"

Hilde didn't say a word, but Miss Sanderson corrected Clementine's English. "Clementine, when wearing ladylike clothes, your grammar should match. The correct thing to say is, 'Isn't that pretty?' And then, even Hilde would agree."

"All righty, then. Hilde, do you see my *pretty* hat? Do you know what color it is? Scarlet! Me, Clementine Earlene Clark, sporting something as high-falutin' as dove gray and scarlet red."

Clementine couldn't contain her laughter. She kicked both heels in the air, which may have been a spectacle. Whenever she'd previously ridden to town with her brothers, on a load of lumber, all dressed like one of them, they called her Clem. That saved the men from explaining to others that they didn't have a clue how to dress a kid sister. The men at the docks and lumberyards naturally thought she was just one of the Clark boys.

"I can't pass for a man now, Hilde gal, and I'd never want to! Even Old Floss and Blossom won't recognize me except I've gotta wear my boots to do chores in, even though Saylor said boot wearin' should be done in private or not at all. So, I'll do it before the fellas come home."

CHAPTER TWO

"If you're afraid of butter, use cream."

Julia Child

Heath and Hardy were the first to wash up for supper. They stepped into the cabin, happy to see bowls of stew on the table and a fresh strawberry pie cooling in the windowsill. "Sis must've gotten home okay," Hardy remarked.

"Li'l Sis?" Heath called. "Did you have fun shopping in town today?"

Clementine waited in her room like a stage actress, ready to make a grand entrance. Just then, Matthew and Pete barreled through the back door. "Smells good," Pete cried. They washed up too and took their places around the table.

"Pie?" Matthew asked. "What's the celebration?"

"I reckon Clementine's got new shoes and a mirror," Heath said.

"I'm looking in the mirror right now," Clementine called.

"Git on out so we can say grace and eat," Matthew requested. "I could smell supper all the way down to the river!"

"Are you all sitting down?" Clementine asked.

"Ah, Li'l Sis," Hardy moaned. "One shopping trip and

you've turned into a game-playin' woman."

Clementine took a shivery breath to control her excitement, and into the kitchen she walked. Four hungry mouths fell right open. Four sets of eyes bugged from their faces. Four brothers stammered for their words, but it was Heath who cried, "I can't believe you're really a girl! I mean—a womanly kind of a girl."

"Li'l Sis is well on to twenty-six. That makes her a woman proper, I reckon," Matthew said.

"Twenty bucks goes farther than I thought," Pete observed, still shocked to see his sister resembling the very kind of creatures he sometimes dreamed about.

"That woman from the newspaper, Saylor Sanderson? She came along first thing, and she just sort of took over my appointment at the women's shop. And the next thing I knew, I was being fitted for dainty underthings, and was fully coordinated because it was Saylor's dream to do that. So she spent a chunk of her own money on me, but she said it wasn't charity. She's the purtiest lady in the world, fellas—and she has the loveliest innards ever."

"Matches her outards," Hardy teased. He'd never enjoyed reading the newspaper more in his life.

"Sis, you do Ma proud," Matthew said, still marveling. "Better take a turn so we can see you from every angle."

The doting older brothers whistled and cheered, complimenting Clementine in every way possible throughout supper. And then Heath said, "Now, tomorrow you must take it all back."

"But why?" Clementine wailed. "Saylor promised it wasn't charity, but her soul's desire—next to Andy, that is."

"Because you're sure to leave us now. Who can make

better pie than you? Who would ever cook for us and clean up after us better than you, Li'l Sis? Nope, it's all gotta go back. This was a rash mistake."

The brothers laughed, and inside, Clementine cheered because Heath had good taste, and he was worried that she might actually be marketable. "I'm glad you were teasing," Clementine said. "For a minute, I was afraid you were serious."

Heath sighed. "I can't strip your possibilities away from you now, but we'll miss ya."

Clementine laughed. "Ah, Heath, I ain't gone nowheres yet!"

That very night, while the Clarks were sleeping— Clementine in her parents' old bedroom near the kitchen, and Heath, Hardy, Matthew, and Pete snoring in the loft upstairs—someone slipped a letter under the door. Clementine was up the earliest. It was her job to milk Flossy and Blossom, and to care for Hilde and the hens. She found the envelope on the mat and stooped to get it. *Miss Clementine Clark* was written in lovely cursive.

> *Dearest Lovely Clementine,*
>
> *I must share my greatest happiness with you! Andy and I are getting married tomorrow. I will be vacating my position at the Spruce Telephone Company. I also will be leaving my room at the Lawrence Boarding House, but I've paid my rent to the end of the year, so you won't owe anything till January. You're a bona fide modern now!*
>
> *I'll come for you the day after tomorrow. Now you shall have plenty of places to wear your lovely clothes. Practice your best grammar and*

prepare for your adventures with the Switchboard Sisterhood.

Sincerely,

Saylor

"Gosh all Friday, poor Heath won't like the sound of this," Clementine whispered to herself, shocked as all outdoors about her sudden thrust into society. "I better cook a hearty breakfast and tell him after his second cup of coffee." Then Clementine drew the letter to her chest and sighed. "But I'm gonna *be* somebody!"

She explained things to Floss and Blossom and they switched their tails from side to side, giddy with excitement. "Are you in udder amazement?" she asked, finding her pun funny. They were agreeable enough, and the hens clucked their congratulations. Hilde brayed a hee and a haw. So, with barnyard encouragement, she went to the house. She strained the cream from the milk, and then poured the cream into the butter churn. She turned the crank handle around and around, and whenever her arm got tired, she'd switch hands. Soon enough, however, butter was born of her efforts. Clementine washed and salted the butter before patting it into a pretty butter mold that was once her mother's. Heath said Ma had always referred to her creamy yellow butter as "Alaskan gold."

Clementine then set straight away to cooking breakfast. After the bacon was done sizzling, she cracked fresh eggs into a large cast-iron skillet. She made flapjacks, and just as the meal was ready to serve, her brothers came down the ladder from their bedroom loft. "Smells delicious," Pete said.

"Thanks, Li'l Sis," Hardy added. "You sure work hard."

"If you men aren't careful, women will run the world," Clementine said.

The guys laughed, but Clementine rehearsed the old adage, "Men work from sun to sun, but a woman's work is never done."

Pete said grace, and the happy chatter of breakfast began. Clementine kept their cups full of coffee, and just as Heath patted his satisfied belly, scooting his chair away from the table, she said, "Fellas, I've had a correspondence from town—"

"Correspondence?" Pete asked. "Well, listen to that! She gets all gussied up one day, and on the very next, she uses some high-falutin' word for mail!" Matthew joined him in a hearty chuckle.

Clementine waded through their goading, saying, "I'm packin' up my things today. I will begin work at the Spruce Telephone Company and shall take Saylor Sanderson's room at the Lawrence Boarding House." She held her breath because all the laughter and gaiety stopped midstream. The Clark brothers were just as dumbstruck as Clementine had been earlier. She looked toward Heath, the brother she was the very closest to, uttering a pensive, "Please—"

"Li'l Sis," Heath said, with tears gathering in his eyes, "I could never stop you if it's what you really want." He opened his arms, and Clementine rushed into them just as she had done so many times as a girl. "I'm gosh-dern proud of you. Of course you may go, if it's what you really want."

"With me out of the way now, you might all consider getting wives to do the grunt work around here," Clementine replied.

"Nobody can cook like you—or grunt like you," Matthew

teased. "I like livin' in the bachelorhood."

"You won't like it nearly as well when you are the one milkin' the cow and makin' the butter," Hardy interjected. "Town's gettin' the better end of this deal! I want my five dollars back."

Of course, Hardy was the oldest of the twins, but somehow Heath had emerged as the natural-born leader of the family after Pa died. What Heath said was the direction things generally went. He'd given Clementine his blessing, and the others had no choice but to follow suit.

"I'll do the washin' and shine things up real nice today, then I'll go out and see if I can shoot somethin' for supper. I'll treat you fellas real nice for all you've done for me."

"We're all gonna have to git wives now. It'll take one or two a piece to make up for you, Li'l Sis," Pete said glumly.

"Best worker in the bunch," Matthew agreed.

"And the best shot," Hardy admitted to the delight of his brothers. It was true. Clementine was a crack shot! It had always made Pa so proud that his little blondie could outshoot her older brothers.

Clementine set to work straight away, clearing breakfast and wiping the table. She heated some water on the Monarch cookstove, and washed and dried the dishes. She decided to make a celebratory custard, since she had plenty of cream and plenty of eggs. It made the whole cabin smell good as it baked. Clementine scrubbed clothes and bedsheets and hung them out to dry. She watered the squash plants with rinse water.

She picked a few peas, dropping pods in her pocket to munch on as she hunted, then she took Pa's shotgun and went out to see what she could find. Luckily, she was able to get a nice rabbit. Heath's favorite meal was rabbit pie, so Clementine walked back through the trees and matted grass to the house, dressed the rabbit, and got it into a pot. Then she went out and pulled carrots from the garden. She picked a few more peas and shelled them, and washed several little pearl onions. Soon enough, Clementine had a flavorful, bubbling stew to pour inside a flaky, buttery crust.

And all that day as she washed, worked, hunted, cooked, and packed her new things inside Ma's old suitcase, she dreamed about having herself a career. What would it be like? Could she learn better grammar, as Saylor encouraged her to do? She wondered if the other ladies would have pretty clothes too, and if they'd be half as kind as Saylor. It was certain nobody could be as generous, but if only they were half as kind, Clementine felt she would be okay.

"It ain't *purty*, 'tis *pretty*," she coached herself. "And it ain't *ain't,* but *isn't.*" She set the table, using one of Ma's nicest tablecloths. It was a special occasion. By the time the men came home, the house was scrubbed and gleaming.

"Ain't that somethin'!" Matthew said. "It's purty enough to be Sunday."

"*Isn't* it something?" Clementine said, trying so hard to implement Saylor's good English. "It *is pretty* enough to be Sunday, and yet we know that it's not. Now, wash up proper."

"Well, la-dee-da and da-tee-da, Miss High-Falutin' Gal," Mathew growled, but he washed up proper because he was hungry enough to eat his arm.

Hardy, Heath, Matthew, and Pete complimented Clementine again and again on the quality of their supper. During the happy clatter of the meal, Clementine forgot herself and said, "I outdone myself on this pie. I ain't never made better!"

Heath raised his glass of cold milk high in the air and cried, "To Li'l Sis! I'll be gosh-derned if it ain't the best meal we ever et."

The brothers were excited for their little sister to move forward, finding a life of her own, and they knew this would probably start a chain reaction for all of them. "When I find me a gal, Li'l Sis, you gotta teach her how to cook like this," Hardy said. "Cuz I don't think they make 'em like you anymore."

CHAPTER THREE

"There's no use trying to pass a Ford, because there is always another one just up ahead."

Henry Ford

Saylor and Andy came as promised the next morning. Clementine was packed and ready to go. She'd hugged her brothers goodbye earlier, claiming they all knew where they could find her. "I'll come home once in a while and cook for you," she promised. "Maybe we can go shootin'."

Mr. Ashton loaded her suitcase in record time. He seemed somewhat distracted. Perhaps being newly married had something to do with it. "Congratulations," Clementine offered. Saylor was affable, gushing over Clementine's ensemble, still seeing her as a glorious transformation.

The drive to the Lawrence Boarding House was a quick one. Andy had a lead foot on the throttle. There must have been some leftover honeymooning on his mind. He even parked fast. Clementine drew a deep breath. The house was three stories tall, and painted purple with yellow trim. "One thing's for certain—I won't confuse it with any of the other homes on this street," Clementine said.

"It's ghastly," Saylor agreed. "It reminds me of a big bruise."

"I was thinkin' more along the lines of one gigantic

pansy," Clementine offered generously.

Saylor pointed out the wraparound porch. "The Switchboard Sisterhood likes to spend their evenings entertaining beaus out here."

"Doin' what?" Clementine quizzed.

"Listening to the phonograph, just talking as they swing." There were two large porch swings that looked rather fun. Clementine wondered what she'd ever chat about with a beau.

The women entered the front hall, and Saylor motioned the way to the stairs. They began the ascent, heels clicking pleasantly on the steps. "We sound like a typewriter," Clementine observed, making Saylor laugh.

Andy passed them on the steps, having already delivered the suitcase to Clementine's new room. "I'll be out in the car," he said in a rush.

"I reckon he's excited to be rid of me today," Clementine observed.

"Oh, he's all right," Saylor said congenially, not wanting to hurry her new friend. "This is your room," she said. "I left you a mirror—and this rug. Miss Reynolds is your roommate. She does calisthenics every night, if you want to join her."

"I don't hold one religion over another," Clementine said, making Saylor giggle. "As long as she don't expect me to join her in the Catholicstenics, I don't mind a bit."

"*Doesn't,*" Saylor corrected, then she said, "and that was *calisthenics*, which just means…exercise. You know, sit-ups and things."

"Oh, well, see how I misunderstood that?" Clementine guffawed. "Whenever we talk about exercise back home, we just say it the way it is. And the way it usually is…is Indian leg wrestles. I can still flip Pete."

"Well, for Pete's sake," Saylor chided playfully. "So, is flipping Pete your religion?"

Clementine had a good sense of humor, so she laughed heartily at Saylor's joke and the whole misunderstanding in general. Saylor led Clementine through the rest of the house. She showed her the dining room, library, and parlor, which the Lawrences shared with their boarders. "Gentleman callers must be gone by nine each evening, and boarders must be in by ten o'clock sharp or you'll be locked out. And no matter what you do, no matter how hungry you are, don't touch old Jethro's cookies."

Clementine was to learn that Mr. Guy Lawrence managed Archer Merchandise, the store where she'd purchased her own full-length mirror that she'd left back home in the cabin. Jethro Lawrence was his aging father, and Guy's wife was Ethel Lawrence. Ethel enjoyed baking and bragged that she made the best pies around. Clementine secretly made it a goal to challenge that fact at some point, but to the mistress of the manor, she said only, "Lemon meringue is my favorite."

Mrs. Lawrence produced Saylor's old boarding contract, and the lease was changed to Clementine's name. Saylor made sure it said in writing that the rent was paid up for the remainder of the year. All these things took a little bit of time, and when the ladies finally made their way down the porch steps, poor Mr. Ashton was swinging his pocket watch and sighing heavily.

"Boy, that took forever," he complained.

"Formalities," Saylor breezed coolly, not one bit rattled by her husband's impatient antics. It seemed to Clementine that Saylor liked them.

"And now it's off to the Spruce Telephone Company, eh?"Andy asked as helped the women into the car and then zoom, he backed onto the street. Saylor squealed delightedly, but before the Model T went very far down the street, Andy was pulled over by the sheriff. "I don't have time for this," Andy muttered.

The lawman sauntered up to the automobile, not in any hurry at all. "You're going kind of fast," he said.

"Yes, I am in a hurry," Andy explained. "Now I'm in a bigger hurry." He seemed to be getting a headache.

The sheriff peered around, nodding to the newly wedded Mrs. Ashton, who beamed a radiant smile if only to soften the encounter. "Congratulations on your marriage," Sheriff Martin said. He slapped Andy on his back, making the young driver bristle.

Sheriff Martin then saw Clementine in the back seat. He tipped his hat and said, "Oh, hello there, pretty lady."

"Me?" Clementine asked, looking at the empty space next to her on the seat. Of course he must have meant her, but she'd never been addressed as a lady before, let alone a purty one!

The lawman jutted his hand toward her, saying, "Sheriff Roy Martin. Pleased to meet you."

Clementine blushed a shade to match her red high heels, but Andy said, "Please, Sheriff, I haven't time for small talk!" His impatience saved Clementine the need for words.

"Now, listen, young man. You should just slow down," the lawman cried. "There's no excuse for running all over Anchorage at twice the speed of sanity!"

Andy's head angled hotly, and Clementine expected fisticuffs at any moment, but darling Saylor leaned over and rubbed Andy's neck, saying soothing sweet nothings in his ear. His posture softened by a league. Then Saylor leaned over to make eye contact with the lawman, saying, "Thank you for the good warning, Sheriff Martin. We'll take it easy!"

And just like that, Andy didn't get a ticket. Saylor was such a smooth operator, and Clementine was more than happy to watch her manipulate things and people. "This has been the most exciting day of my life," Clementine gasped as they pulled away from the curb. "I can say I've been part of a high-speed chase!"

"That was hardly high speed," Saylor said.

"Furthermore, it was not a chase," Andy added.

Still, the whole scene was enough to put butterflies in Clementine's stomach. Old Hilde never done that.

The Spruce Telephone Company loomed large. Clementine had never contemplated a career before she met Saylor. It was an unattainable thing. Now, here she stood on the precipice, as it were, of a new beginning. She took a deep breath as Saylor linked arms with her and marched her right up the steps and inside the two-story building.

Clementine noticed a portrait of Lester the Moose. He was the second most-photographed celebrity in Anchorage, and Saylor Sanderson was the first. Even out-of-towners like the Clarks knew all about the shaggy old nuisance.

"That's a nice picture of Lester," Clementine said before Saylor dragged her over to a desk.

"Mrs. Julie Tremblay, I'd like you to meet Clementine Clark."

"Yes, we've been expecting you," the officially employed woman said. Wow, a modern, right here before Clementine's very eyes!

"Oh, that makes me sound important!"

"We value all our ladies, Miss Clark. You are all important to us."

Clementine didn't know what more to say. She shifted her weight awkwardly. Mrs. Tremblay congratulated Saylor on her wedding and handed her a gift. Just then, a puny man came through the door, carrying the most immodest bouquet of flowers imaginable. The distraction saved Clementine from trying to generate small talk.

"A delivery for Miss Helen Gagnon," the florist said from somewhere inside the arrangement.

"Sit them right there," Mrs. Tremblay instructed. "Oh, this is so exciting for Helen! She's never had flowers delivered here before."

Suddenly Mr. Tremblay burst from his office, saying, "No! Saylor, *you* take the flowers! I can't afford losing any more operators!"

Now Mrs. Tremblay's cheeks reddened with embarrassment. To think her own husband would say such a thing in front of a new prospect! "This is Miss Clark," Julie said, and she may as well have said it in pig latin because it meant many things, like "Hush, and watch yourself, man! You don't want to frighten Saylor's replacement away."

Jason Tremblay righted himself quickly, inviting Clementine inside his private office. He pointed to a chair, and she nervously sat down. "I'm Jason Tremblay," he offered officially. "I do most of the hiring and the firing around here. For some reason, however, Mr. Otto

Lloyd, the company owner, has called me regarding his wishes for your employment. You are to replace Miss Sanderson—er, Mrs. Ashton—forthwith."

"Oh," Clementine said, wishing she understood the true power of new shoes. It all sounded so wonderfully important! And a word like "forthwith." What could get better than that?

"So, you have already secured your position here," Mr. Tremblay said, studying the woman closer.

Clementine seemed terribly wide-eyed and innocent for one so pretty and smartly dressed. Miss Clark was a looker, but where were her feminine flapping wiles? Her large eyes swept around the office, trying to light on a topic of conversation.

Mr. Tremblay interceded her need to speak by speaking more himself. He said, "And you're not engaged, not with child, and not courting anyone seriously, are you?"

"Mercy, no! I ain't engaged, and I ain't with child!"

"Aren't," the man amended.

"I *aren't* with child," Clementine defended again. Boy, these townies were a brassy bunch! And nitpicky when it came to grammar.

"Well, in your case, you should say, 'I'm not with child,' etcetera."

"I ain't, I aren't, and *I'm not* with child, etcetera!" Clementine declared with conviction. What kinds of moral dilemmas did he expect?

Mr. Tremblay smiled. Clementine Clark was naïve to her own allure—and even to the opportunities life would throw her way. He hated to label her as a dumb blonde, but this rustic innocence would be a precious boon to the phone company. Perhaps this one would stay around a while and really make a career out of the switchboard.

"Welcome to the Spruce Telephone Company!" He thrust his hand forward, and Clementine pumped it up and down heartily. "Now, you take yourself upstairs and find Helen or Hazel Gagnon. I'm warning you, they are twins, so you really will be seeing double. They will get you trained."

"You mean I'm a bona fide official working woman?"

Mr. Tremblay glanced at his watch. "You are on the clock," he said. He showed her how to punch a timecard, and Clementine went up the steps, one at a time, to face the fate of a telephone switchboard operator. Saylor was no longer there to push her, prod her, or drag her.

CHAPTER FOUR

"The most effective way to do it is to do it."

Amelia Earhart

Helen and Hazel were red-headed twins, and they had worked for the company the longest. "I reckon you know everything there is to know," Clementine said, making Helen smile. "I hope you won't mind my takin' notes."

Helen was impressed that the stylish little thing was willing to listen and write things down. "Being teachable is a preferred quality. Sit down here," Helen said, leading her to her chair at the switchboard. Several other ladies were patching calls in and out. Clementine had a difficult time not listening to them instead of Helen's instructions.

"It's noisy, like the continuatin' buzz of a beehive," she said.

"I like that description," Helen said. "You're quite right, but 'continuatin'' isn't a word."

"It ain't?"

"No, it *isn't*. You are looking for 'continuous' or 'continual' in this sense."

"At least I got part of it right," Clementine defended. "The 'continu' part."

Helen smiled wryly. Of course, she had received the monstrous bouquet of flowers earlier, and from her favorite, most admired columnist, Charlie Blaze. Perhaps that had something to do with her congenial mood. It seemed the willowy operator could do little but smile at the new girl and appreciate the funny things she said.

When Helen went downstairs, one of the ladies said, "Helen sure has been in a good mood since those flowers showed up."

"They were bigger than the man that brung 'em," Clementine declared, pleased to have been a witness to the delivery.

"I'm Roxy," the pleasant brunette said between calls.

"Oh! You're my roommate," Clementine said. "Saylor said I could have no kinder roommate in all the world than you, and that the two of us," she motioned between Roxy and herself, "could be *good* friends, but we can never be *best* friends because you and Saylor are *best* friends."

"That's very generous of her," Roxy whispered before patching another call.

"Is this job hard?" Clementine asked an operator named Vivian.

"It can be challenging sometimes. When folks want 'information' and we don't have it—that's a little disarming."

Clementine's chin dropped. "How's a person s'posed to know what the answers are?"

Roxy finished transferring a call and answered, "Well, we make it a practice to know general things, such as what the specials are at the local cafés, things like that."

Just then, someone called and demanded "information." Roxy calmly checked a chart in front of her and said,

"Yes, it's 9:00 p.m. in London, England, right now. They are nine hours ahead of us in Alaska."

Clementine was all eyes and all ears. Roxy Reynolds handled the situation beautifully! Oh, to speak so calmly, to have such a gentle demeanor! Clementine couldn't think of a better person to be like under pressure, and she said so.

Roxy smiled. "I don't get fussed up about stuff."

"That's what Saylor said, too."

Another of the operators cast a look in Roxy and Clementine's direction. It meant, "Hush up and go to work." Roxy was quick to dodge back into her duties. Clementine simply watched what was happening. She wasn't yet allowed to answer a call without Helen's tutelage.

When Helen returned, she wasn't Helen at all, but Hazel. Since Hazel *hadn't* received flowers, Clementine determined to be on her best behavior. Hazel showed her some things, and then she said, "Here you go." The board lit up. "Answer it."

Clementine's heart raced. Was she supposed to say "Operator" or "Information?" She cast a troubled look over her shoulder and Hazel prompted her, saying, "How may I connect your call?"

With a shaky voice, Clementine said, "How may I connect your call?"

A man's voice on the other end of the line said, "How much wood could a woodchuck chuck if a woodchuck could chuck wood?"

"Oh," Clementine cried happily. "I know this one!" Her energetic response brought stares from the other operators, and slight tongue-tsking from Helen, but Clementine replied, "The answer is 700 pounds if the wind was at his back! So much wood would a woodchuck chuck as a woodchuck would if a woodchuck could chuck wood!"

The caller hung up without argument. "I knew that one," Clementine repeated.

"What was the question?" Helen asked, brows furrowed.

"You know, the old thing about how much wood would a woodchuck chuck if a woodchuck could chuck wood. And I'm something of an old woodchuck myself."

"What kind of a lunatic bothered you for that?" an operator named Florence quizzed.

"A drunk one," Morganna guessed.

"Well, I hope he calls back," Clementine said, feeling personally validated. From now on, she vowed to stop comparing herself so much to the other ladies. Clementine Clark knew stuff too!

The walk home was rather cheery. Clementine listened to the pocketsful of conversation, happy to have friends. Roxy was extra kind to include her in some of the talk as well. "Tell us about yourself," she urged.

"I was ten years old when Pa died. Ma passed when I was just a baby. I've been mostly raised by older brothers."

"Are they handsome?" one of the ladies asked.

"I reckon they are," Clementine answered shyly. "Especially Heath."

"You'll have to invite them to dinner one night," Vivian teased.

"And send Mrs. Lawrence into a tizzy fit?" Florence

asked. "You'd better not. That's an unreasonable number of mouths to feed."

"Well, if anyone wants to meet my brothers, I'll fetch you home on a weekend. I don't mind cookin' for a crew."

"That's very kind," Roxy said. "You are both generous and genuine. Those are two of my favorite traits in a friend."

"Are you interested in goin' home with me?" Clementine asked, pleased by Roxy's attention.

"I'm not in the market for men just yet, but I do believe you can cook."

"Have you had your heart broke?" Clementine pressed.

"Yes. Yes, my dearest Clementine, that is one way to put it."

"Not me. I never had a beau—never even had a date before, but earlier today, Mr. Tremblay asked me if I was with child. I was a tidbit kerfuffled since I ain't never even smoked a cigarette before, let alone been in a family way."

"The two are not connected," Florence said, and an eyeroll was possibly involved.

"What?" Roxy asked. "That doesn't sound like Mr. Tremblay."

"So, I said, 'No, I ain't.' Then he said, 'Aren't,' so then I said, 'No I aren't.' So, then he said, 'In your case, you would say, 'No, I am not, etcetera.' So, then I said, 'I ain't, I aren't, and I'm *not* pregnant—etcetera!'"

"There must be some mistake," Vivian said. "Mr. Tremblay would never speak in such an accusatory way."

Clementine stopped, examining herself all the way down

the front of her dress. "I mean, is it the navy chiffon that makes me look ready to calve out?"

"Heavens, no," Ruby said. "You look better than Coco Chanel."

Clementine had no idea who Coco Chanel was, but it did sound a might delicious. "Thanks," she answered, adding Ruby to her new list of lifetime friends. "The shoes—they don't make me look fast and loose, do they? I mean, I know they are empowerin' cuz Saylor said so, but they haven't empowered me *that* far, right?"

"The shoes are enviable," Tracy offered. "Did you get them at Archer Merchandise?"

"No, Ashton's Women's Shop."

"That place looks expensive."

"Every place is *really* expensive," Clementine agreed, "but I hit a sale that was a humdinger. I only went in there with twenty dollars, and I came out like all this. Plus, what you'll see me wearin' tomorrow. I've got a different *ensemble* all lined up."

Roxy shook her head. "Sounds like Saylor was being generous. I'm not sure we can call that a sale."

The conversation buzzed like that all the way to the three-story boarding house. "Home sweet home," Florence called. "I hope Mrs. Lawrence made chicken and dumplings for supper."

"I don't care what she made. The walk home has been really nice," Clementine said, so happy to have friends and a career. "I mean, I was worried about what we'd talk about, but the pleasant chatter just continuated all the way."

"'Continuated,'" Florence repeated, perhaps unkindly,

but nobody corrected Clementine's grammar. They were all too hungry.

The banter around the dinner table was nice, and it helped Clementine feel less homesick. As soon as the meal was over, however, many of the ladies drifted out to the porch to visit with their beaus and gentlemen callers. Clementine had no such inducement, and it felt wrong to walk away from the table without helping with dishes. So, she scurried up to her room and grabbed her best apron, tied it around her waist, and surprised the living daylights out of Mrs. Lawrence.

"What's this, then?" Ethel asked.

"Thought I might as well help. I have no other plans, and it will make me feel useful."

Grandpa Jethro Lawrence smiled at that. Apparently, he was the scullery maid around here, always helping with dishes and cleanup. He grinned approvingly, sitting himself in a corner rocking chair.

"I have no money to pay you," Mrs. Lawrence said skeptically.

"I'll give her a cookie if she does a proper job," Jethro said.

Clementine laughed. "I have no need for payment, but land sakes, Mrs. Lawrence, you feed a lot of mouths around here. Let me help when I can."

"Givin' this gal two cookies," Jethro said. "I like her better than the last fancy flibbertigibbet, whoever she was."

"You don't mean Saylor Sanderson?" Clementine quizzed. She felt her eyebrows shoot high. How could anyone in the world prefer her over Saylor? "I can't figure that one."

The old man stroked his chin thoughtfully. "A couple of the gals baked me cookies for my hundredth birthday. They baked me one for every year of my life, and that little scamp tried helpin' herself to some of them in the middle of the night."

Clementine laughed out loud. She liked Jethro. His grammar was aligned with her own. "You sure don't look a hundred," she said.

"He's not a hundred! I doubt if he's eighty," Ethel scoffed.

"Hush yourself, daughter," Jethro said. "Or I'll make you milk the cow your own self."

"You have a cow?" Clementine asked.

"I couldn't afford to feed everyone otherwise. We keep a cow and about thirty chickens," Mrs. Lawrence explained.

"I can milk her if you need me to."

Ethel looked at Clementine like she had won the jackpot. "Truthfully, I'd rather milk than wash the dishes."

"I don't blame you there," Clementine said. "What's your cow's name?"

"Contessa," Grandpa Jethro answered.

Clementine smiled at Mrs. Lawrence. "All righty, then. You milk, I'll wash, and Jethro can dry."

Ethel seemed thrilled to escape the hot kitchen, but Jethro grumbled under his breath until the last dish was put away. When Mrs. Lawrence came back into the kitchen, Clementine washed the milk dishes, too.

"You are not spoiled, are you, Miss Clark?" Ethel asked.

"I have been utterly spoiled, Mrs. Lawrence. You see, I've never gone without a meal once in my life—and even after I lost Pa, I still had brothers who cared about me. I'm just hopin' they are doin' okay tonight. Hope somebody remembered to milk old Floss and Blossom. Hope the fellas remember to wash the milk buckets. I've doted on them proper for a while."

"I'm sure they are missing you, dear, but it won't hurt them a bit to do for themselves—maybe they'll even decide they need wives!" Mrs. Lawrence chuckled.

Roxy taught night school two nights a week at the municipal building. Judging by her kind character, Clementine imagined she was a wonderful teacher. She came in just as Clementine was putting away the last of her things.

"Only one suitcase?" Roxy asked. "Saylor had five steamer trunks. Five! It took me six nights to help her put her things away, and on the seventh, she up and got married." Both ladies laughed.

"Saylor said if boots must be worn, I should never let anyone see me in them. It's just as well. They were Pete's old ones."

"I have boots—I figured I might find a horse to ride sometime."

"Have you?"

"Not yet." Roxy sighed, drawing laughter from Clementine. "But a girl can have her dreams."

"You're from Wyoming, right?"

"Yes, indeed I am—from the southwestern corner."

"What's it like?"

"It's much less green than Alaska. You have trees—we have sagebrush. You have coastlines and big fishing industries—we have antelope and rocky fossil buttes. You have lumberjacks and gold miners—we have cowboys and coalminers."

"We have oceans and inlets and rivers—with big old salmon," Clementine said, stretching her arms to illustrate the size.

"We have creeks and streams and tributaries—and some nice brook trout." Roxy's hands drew about ten inches apart.

Clementine smiled at the brunette across the room. She was especially interested when Roxy got down on the rug and did those...exercises. "Saylor said you do this each night."

"Calisthenics is good for the heart, I think."

"So are Indian leg wrestles. I'd give it a go with you sometime if you wanted. Ya know, the secret is all in the leveragin' and not brute force."

"I've got nothing to prove." Roxy laughed. "But you're an original, Clementine Clark, through and through."

The curvaceous blonde flashed a sincere smile. "That's just what Heath says about me, too."

"We're going to get along just fine," Roxy said, turning out the light.

CHAPTER FIVE

"He looked at her the way all women want to be looked at by a man."

The Great Gatsby

A few weeks later, the ladies were walking home after the day shift when they heard someone yell for help. The gals peered over the edge of the ravine that existed near the corner of Cook and Third Streets. There was Sheriff Roy Martin, clinging for dear life to the top of a pine tree. "Help! Lester's gone rutting—he's left the gully."

"Then why are you up the tree that way?" Clementine asked.

"Bears," he said, pointing down. The ladies squealed and scattered, but Clementine peered over the edge, taking stock of the situation. The bears were each playing with a mirror that Saylor had hung in Lester's boudoir. The mirrors had entertained Lester into vanity, and he'd quit harassing the ladies as they walked to and from work each day.

"Hold on," Clementine said. She jogged to the lawman's truck and grabbed a rifle. "Want me to shoot them?" she asked.

"No, just see if you can scare them away," the man said.

"I meant the mirrors." Clementine squeezed off a shot, and one mirror shattered to bits, leaving the bear quite confuzzled. The sow dropped down to all fours, trying to figure out where her reflection had gone. Clementine aimed again, shooting the second mirror. That bear was puzzled as well, but when the sow couldn't figure things out, she ambled back over to the pine tree that Sheriff Martin clung to and began shaking the trunk.

"It seems she's as content with one plaything as another," Clementine observed pleasantly.

Sheriff Martin whimpered a meek reply.

"Oh, don't fret none," Clementine said, popping the old gal right in the bloomers. The grizzly yowled indignantly, and both bears scrambled through the trees, making their way up the north slope until they were well out of sight.

"You're quite a shot," Florence said to Clementine. Once the first shot had been fired, the women gathered back to watch the unfolding spectacle.

"Well done," Roxy said, clapping Clementine's shoulder. "Good thinking!"

The others cheered as Roy Martin climbed successfully down the tree and back up to the embankment on the road where they stood. Clementine handed him his gun and said, "Here ya go."

"It's not every day our city gains an unlikely hero," he said, appraising Clementine Clark with renewed interest. "Especially one as pretty as you, little lady."

"You probably say that to all your heroes," Clementine teased, then she turned quickly before her cheeks blushed a shade to match her red shoes. "See ya in the funny papers, Sheriff."

The women laughed about the incident the rest of the way home.

"The poor man," Tracy teased. "Scared by bears and saved by a woman."

"That's the way to represent the fairer sex, Clementine. We'll prove we are stronger by far," Florence said.

"There's two things my brothers say every woman should know how to do," Clementine remarked. "How to shoot and how to surrender, and to know which one to apply at the critical moment."

Roxy grinned. Sometimes that backwards-talking woodsy woman made a lot of good sense! When Roxy got home, she dialed Hank Pendleton from *The Anchorage Times*. "Clementine deserves some recognition. Saylor surely made the front page for hanging the mirrors in Lester's gulch in the first place. It brought much needed peace to the town! But the fellow was out rutting, and bears moved in and tried turning his bedchambers into a circus funhouse."

It took only fifteen minutes for the reporter to knock on the Lawrences' door. He began actively salivating as Clementine came downstairs, still owning her red shoes and fun plaid number like nobody's business. The shameless reporter whistled slightly and said, "Hi ya, doll!"

Clementine turned to see who was coming down the stairs behind her, but to her surprise there wasn't a soul. She scrunched her brows quizzically, never understanding her beauty. Vanity was the furthest thing from Clementine's character.

Mr. Pendleton continued, "I hear you saved the sheriff's life today."

"I don't know about that," Clementine answered modestly. "But I shot the shoot out of Lester's mirrors, and the bears run off."

"Ran," Roxy corrected.

"I'll have to replace the mirrors because I never intended to undo nothin' that Saylor done."

"Did," Roxy coached from a few paces away.

Clementine bit her lip, wondering what more she could add. "I s'pect Lester will be pretty steamed when he comes back to town and finds his mirrors all broke up like that. However, I also s'pose it proves moose are generally better mannered than bears."

"Yes, I s'pose it does," the reporter agreed, milking the interview for his own personal entertainment, if nothing more.

"I'll replace the mirrors," Guy Lawrence called, hearing the hullaballoo. "I'll send the bill to the sheriff's office because I am a good businessman."

"That will show him," Florence said from somewhere in the house, making Roxy giggle. That Florence—she had a way.

"Miss Clark," the reporter pressed, "do you think Mr. Tremblay would let me borrow you for a little while tomorrow? I'd like to reenact the scene."

"Maybe," Clementine said, voice full of wonder. Then she kindly softened her expression to squelch over-lofty expectations of the journalist. "I don't s'pose we could round those sows up for another go. I popped one of them right in the bloomers." She couldn't help rubbing her own bottom as she said it.

"Oh, to be so beautifully dumb," Florence breathed, making Roxy giggle harder.

"We'll leave the bears out of it," Hank Pendleton replied, trying hard to discipline his own delighted expression.

"Well," Clementine hedged, eyes waltzing right around in a circle. "Pardon me for noticing this, but it just won't seem as dangerous, what with the sheriff clinging to the top of the pine tree that way, and nothin' below him but a bunch of broken glass."

"I do appreciate your consideration for my feelings," Hank said, chortling into his fist as he did so. "And we shall just have to do our best. Tomorrow, yes?"

"Yes," Clementine agreed. "Well, thanks for comin' by."

"Would you be interested in a little stroll, Miss Clark?"

Oh, dear. Clementine's heart practically stopped midbeat. "Where would we stroll to?" she asked. "I was just going to help Mrs. Lawrence set the table for supper."

"Might I call back in an hour?"

"Yes, I s'pose that would be all right."

"I'll be back soon then," the man said. He tipped his hat and left, leaving Clementine in a panic. Some of the ladies tried to coach her on strolls and how to enjoy them.

"I'm twenty-six, but I just never learned about this stuff," she confessed.

Tracy said, "You won't learn any younger. I think it's exciting! He's a reporter, you know."

"Yes. Funny how Roxy is engaged to a journalist—you know, Reese Remington—and now I've been asked to go walking around with a newspaperman. These typewriter types are fast movers."

Vivian giggled merrily. "Oh, Clementine! You crazy gal—I wouldn't call a garden stroll an engagement."

"I certainly hope not. I can't go marrying the first one of these men I walk with. What would Mr. Tremblay think of me then? He already suspected me of some pretty serious things, and all I ever done was nothin'."

"It will all work out," Nora said while breezing by. "Florence has been strolling with her beau, Joe, for two years and she's not engaged."

"She should buy him a typewriter," Clementine challenged. "I've promised Mr. Tremblay I'll be a career gal for at least a while longer."

Clementine could scarcely eat her supper, and Mrs. Lawrence was disappointed by her smallish appetite. "I was hoping you were enjoying the oyster stew," she said. "I made those baking powder biscuits fresh this afternoon."

Clementine wasn't a grammar major, but "oyster stew" and "enjoy" were never two things that went together in a sentence. Clementine had never enjoyed the gritty, slimy things.

"The biscuits are especially tasty," she said, loading one up with butter and honey. It was the only way to get the stew beyond her tonsils, and she hated to seem ungrateful. "I must excuse myself tonight without helping," Clementine said. "I have strolling to do."

Mr. Pendleton called precisely at eight. Clementine was ready. She wore her fun plain number and red heels because, to hear Saylor tell it, red shoes were something like the whole armor of God. She wore her red cardigan and topped cloche to match.

Hank offered his arm, and Clementine nervously took hold of it as they went down the porch steps. Her mind was void of things to say when Mr. Pendleton said, "You smell delightful, Miss Clark."

"Oh, well, I doused myself with a little rose water to cover the oysters."

The reporter was unable to conceal his amusement, and a happy chuckle escaped him. "Oysters?" he asked.

"That was what Mrs. Lawrence made for dinner. Had I realized we'd fallen on hard times around here, I'd have gone off and shot a rabbit or something."

Hank laughed again. "Miss Clark, you are as refreshing as a summer rain."

"I hope it won't rain," Clementine said, suddenly eyeing the sky.

"I don't think it will," Hank followed. "I just think *you* are like rain—very refreshing and new."

Clementine didn't know what to say. Both weather and oysters had been thoroughly discussed. The pair walked the perimeter of the Lawrences' property. In the far corner, the milk cow waited near the barn door. "That's Contessa. I milk her sometimes to help out."

"Oh, you know your way around a milk bucket, do you?"

"We keep two cows back home, old Floss and Blossom. They have sweeter cream and that makes better butter, but I haven't said nothin' about it to Mrs. Lawrence. I'd hate to make her feel bad."

"Why is there a difference in the taste?" Hank pressed.

"Well, our cows eat clover and wild grasses growin' along the river. Contessa is stuck in that corner corral eating whatever hay she's fed. For all I know, her fodder is the equivalent of oyster stew."

"What are your interests, Miss Clark?"

"Aside from making butter and cooking? Well, I do enjoy

shopping at Ashton's. Even if I just gaze at them displays in the windows."

"Do you like to read?"

"Yes, I do. I have all Ma's favorite books—but my favorite thing to read is Ma's recipe cards. She had purty penmanship. I like to pretend I know what her voice sounds like when I read the recipes and cook her food."

"Do you care for poetry?" Hank asked. He was good at thinking of things to say, but Clementine didn't know if he was really listening to her answers or just dreaming up questions.

"It depends if they're funny or not."

"Give me an example."

"Well, I'm pretty good at rhymes, even though—to quote my roommate—I lack the finer understandin' of the English language. I mean, I don't know the difference between danglin' participles and nicely rounded diphthongs, but I can—"

Hank Pendleton horn blasted, an irreverent laugh that was apt to curdle Contessa's milk before any could splash into the bucket. Clementine jumped, unaware she'd said any such funny thing.

"Forgive me," Hank said, drawing a long breath. "You are such a funny gal, Clementine. As you were saying, let me hear an extemporaneous rhyme."

"Well, there once was a nun in the cloister who gagged while eating an oyster. She died a hard death, with the fishiest breath, with nary a priest could be found to hoist 'er."

Hank laughed again. He stopped midstride and asked Clementine to repeat the limerick. She did, and he said,

"I think you are spectacular, Miss Clark. How about one more?"

"All righty," Clementine said, finding strolling a bit easier while rhyming things. "There once was a bear with a mirror, and a treed sheriff a tremblin' with fear. I came along, and asked what was wrong, then popped that old sow in the rear."

Hank Pendleton horn blasted a second time, startling Clementine as much as the first, and her flinching was automatic. "I don't think I'm that funny," she said. "And poor Roxy and the others get plenty enough of me."

"You are hilarious, doll. Watcha doin' tomorrow night?"

Clementine ducked bashfully. "Mr. Pendleton, strollin' is one thing, but becomin' engaged lickety-split is somethin' I ain't gonna do. I can't disappoint Mr. Tremblay that way."

"I'm not asking you to get engaged, Miss Clark. I just wondered if you'd like to go dancing."

"Yeah, but you typewriter types are tricky," Clementine said. "You just write yourselves a happy endin'."

"I'll be on my best behavior," the reporter promised.

"I'll have to think on it, Mr. Pendleton."

"Well, since we're back to the porch, I'll bid you goodnight and thank you for a most pleasant time."

"Thanks for the stroll. It was my first ever."

"I'd have never guessed," he called over his shoulder. But under his breath, he repeated, "You typewriter types are tricky."

CHAPTER SIX

"Were it up to me to decide whether we should have
a government without newspapers, or a newspaper
without government, I should not hesitate a moment to
prefer the latter."

Thomas Jefferson

Roxy had slipped out somewhere before the disappointing supper of oyster stew. Since she taught English at night school, and also since she was recently engaged to a writer from *Field & Stream*, Clementine wasn't overly concerned. However, once ten o'clock rolled around and she still hadn't returned, Clementine waged a war between concern for her friend and extreme loyalty to her.

"She might just be carried away, a spoonin' in the moonlight, and I ain't judgy," she said to the pretty blonde girl in the glass. "Maybe I'll get carried away with a reporter of my own after some future, very advanced, modern sort of a stroll."

Clementine knelt down to say her prayers, still concerned about Roxy. "God, I guess I'll just give her to you tonight. I'm afraid if I say somethin', she'll get in trouble with Mr. and Mrs. Lawrence. I don't want to get her in trouble, so you just take care of her."

And then she climbed into bed and slept with the sweetest

dreams that she was home cookin' for her brothers, and when everybody gathered around the table to eat, her folks were there too. It was her favorite dream. Her mother looked just like she did in her wedding picture, and Pa was just as Clementine remembered him. He had the kindest eyes and the kindest smile.

When morning came, Clementine was relieved to see Roxy in her bed, but the tale she told of her night was terrifying! At first Clementine suspected she was tellin' a big whopper, but Roxy wasn't the whopper-tellin' type, and her fatigue was obvious.

"I feel a deep knot of guilt for not organizin' a search party. I didn't want you to get in trouble for violatin' curfew, so I said absolutely nothin' to Mr. Lawrence."

As the story went, Roxy had walked back to the phone company to call her mother in Kemmerer, Wyoming. She hadn't yet told her mother of her forthcoming marriage and felt there wasn't enough privacy at the boarding house.

"You figured right on that account," Clementine said.

But poor Roxanne had forgotten all about the bears they'd seen in Lester's gulch, and they'd returned after dark. As Roxy hurried home in the shadows, she heard the huff of a nearby grizzly and leaped straight off the side of the road, landing atop the same busy pine tree that had earlier cradled the city's sheriff.

"You got yourself in a real fix," Clementine said, listening intently and all the while imagining the awfulness of it.

No help arrived—and nobody knew they should be keeping one eye out. When Mr. Tremblay drove the late evening shift home, they'd motored right by without looking. Hours ticked by, and eventually Roxy prayed she could just be invisible to the bears. Later, she was awakened by her father's voice. He coached her out of the tree until she was safely on the ground and ran for home. "Grandpa Jethro let me in at three this morning. He was up eating cookies and heard me banging."

"I wish I'd have found you so's you could have had a proper night's sleep. I'm sure sorry, Roxy. My brother Heath always told me to listen to my sixth sense, but like I always told him, 'Heath, I ain't got no six cents.'" Roxy smiled blandly, not really appreciating Clementine's humor, but Clementine wasn't offended. Roxy was plum tuckered!

Clementine left Roxy home in bed. "Mr. Tremblay will understand," she said. And of course, the kind manager did. But work was all abuzz over the night's happenings, and at 11:00, Mr. Tremblay drove Clementine to the gully near Third and Cook Streets so the press could reconstruct the happenings. Clementine was happy to see Roxy there with Mr. Pendleton, and who but Saylor was milling around with Sheriff Martin and a couple of rangers.

Hank Pendleton smiled Clementine's way and tipped his hat, but was busy with his camera and notepad. "First of all," Hank said, "take a look down there." He jutted a thumb toward the bottom of the gulch. The two brown bears were busy gazing into two new mirrors.

Saylor grinned happily. "The rangers wondered if the mirrors would bait that set of troublemakers. It worked! Mr. Lawrence and the sheriff hung them early this morning, and an hour ago, they came."

"Now all that's left is for us to relocate them far from here, and there shouldn't be any more trouble," Sheriff Roy Martin declared. "I'm sorry you spent your night the way I spent my afternoon yesterday. I've been in more comfortable trees before," the lawman said to Roxy.

The reporter took pictures while the bears were shot with tranquilizers. They allowed Clementine to do the honors. "That woman is a crack shot," Roy Martin declared, as if the switchboard operator was really Annie Oakley.

Hank Pendleton took pictures of Clementine, Roxy, and Saylor all together. "This makes me feel incorporated," Clementine said.

"Incorporated as what?" Roxy quizzed.

"I don't rightly have it figured," Clementine confessed, "but it feels important and official."

"Of course, you are incorporated into the walking advertisement campaign of Ashton's Women's Shop," Saylor quipped pleasantly. "It's hard to buy this type of publicity! Roxy, you are proof that the strong survive, and Clementine is proof that no woman is too pretty to pack iron. I'm considering a designer line of holsters and scabbards to be seen in the window displays of the store. I believe Anchorage provides the perfect backdrop for that kind of pistol-packing perfection."

"Might I take you to a picnic tonight, Sugar Pie?" the sheriff asked. Hank Pendleton's brows rose upon hearing the request. He had first asked if he could take Clementine dancing, and she'd refused on the grounds of not wanting to "get engaged" and disappointing Mr. Tremblay.

The reporter read her discomfort and said, "She's already promised to go dancing with me, Sheriff, but if you'd like to join us, we'd be pleased."

Clementine scowled. She had not agreed to anything or with anyone! She only knew how to dance with her pa. "I s'pose I can go to the picnic," she said, believing picnicking was less complicated than dancing.

The lawman beamed brightly at his rescuer. "I'll pick

you up from work, if that's all right."

"Well," Hank said, tipping his hat, "you know us typewriter types. I had to be bold enough to try."

"I've got to get back to work now," Clementine said. She hugged Roxy and Saylor and hurried toward Mr. Tremblay's automobile.

The picnic was held at the park just across the street from the municipal building. Clementine was surprised to meet the mayor and several of the city fathers. She was introduced to the Justice of the Peace, Clay Moore, Attorney Anthony Wheelwright, and Mr. Hal Hoskins, the president of the First Bank of Alaska. It was a little starchier affair than most picnics. Altogether, the wives seemed somewhat snooty, but perhaps that's because their husbands were so attentive to the switchboard operator.

"Yes, this is my rescuer. May I present Miss Clementine Clark? Is she a doll cake or what?"

"The pleasure is mine, mine, mine," the mayor cried. "My dear, where did you ever learn to shoot, shoot, shoot?"

Clementine replied, "In the woods, woods, woods, from my pa, pa, pa."

Mrs. Mayor's eyeballs rolled around in a circle and she tsked, tsked, tsked, thinking Clementine to be a vulgar conversationalist. Hal Hoskins came closer, feeling quite proud of his diamond stickpin. "How has such beauty eluded my vision?" the stuffy old curmudgeon asked.

Clementine knew he was a stuffy old curmudgeon because Helen and Hazel always said as much. "That's easy," Clementine replied with wide eyes. "I ain't got no money to give ya."

Now the city fathers and the lawman laughed heartily, very pleased with the answer. The banker did not fancy her reply, and neither did his wife. Mrs. Hoskins tongue-clucked right away. "Poor people have poor ways," she declared.

Clementine didn't care one way or the other. Once they were out of earshot, she asked the sheriff if the First Bank of Alaska had ever been robbed.

"Why, honey, you're not eyeballing it, are you?" he asked. Clementine felt irritated that he should refer to her in so sweet a term, almost as if she didn't have a brain in her head.

"No, Ducky Puddles, I was just curious."

"Who's Ducky Puddles?" Roy Martin quizzed.

"You are."

The man's brows knit oddly. "I'm not Ducky Puddles," he insisted quietly so nearby picnickers couldn't hear.

"I see," Clementine said brightly. "And I am not your honey, your doll cake, *or* your sugar pie. I'm so happy we've cleared up our misunderstandings! Now we shall really enjoy the picnic."

The lawman's forehead creased into lines, but he said only, "Maybe you're only half as sweet as I thought."

"I am a good shot, though," she reminded him, "and I am a solid friend."

"I miss old-fashioned etiquette and the art of feminine subtlety," he grumbled beneath his breath.

"The way that stuffy old curmudgeon goes around showin' off his importance in this town—what with the top hat, overgrown pocket watch, and diamond stickpin glintin' in the sun, he's bound to become a target for lowlifes and thugs."

"Lowlifes and thugs," Sheriff Martin repeated, smiling the smile of a teacher to a child. "Somebody's got a big imagination."

"Well, if it were to be robbed, it would do such a disservice to Mr. Tremblay. He sends Mrs. Tremblay to the bank to make deposits twice weekly on behalf of the Spruce Telephone Company."

"So what?"

"Well, that would be more discouragin' than a passel full of weddin's. And him, tryin' to keep a budget and the bills paid. Why, coal costs alone to heat the buildin' is astronomical."

"Astronomical, phooey! Jason Tremblay's dilemma is no greater than any of the other managers in this town," Roy Martin argued, but not meanly. He seemed to enjoy Clementine's company, even if she did lack subtlety and etiquette. "What about Guy Lawrence's duties for Archer Merchandise? He has even more bills to pay, shelves to stock, and budgets to balance."

"Yes, poor Lawrences," Clementine agreed.

"Ah," Roy Martin said, swatting at the air with one hand like a paw. "There's nothing poor about them, either!"

"Mrs. Lawrence has to keep a milk cow and chickens, or she'd never be able to afford to feed all of us boarders."

"You all pay rent," the lawmen said. "I imagine they are well enough compensated."

"Well, yes, but still, the cost of everything goes up every week. If I was the mayor, I'd say expenses are up, up, up—three ups, just like that." Clementine sighed beneath the weight of so many perceived discouragements.

"Don't worry your pretty head over it," the sheriff said.

"But that's why I hope there's plenty of security at the bank. All of the hardworkin' folks in this town would be plum disrupted if their money got stole."

The sheriff placated his date by patting her shoulder and saying, "There, there. I won't let anyone rob the bank."

Clementine felt annoyed, and wondered if dancing with Hank Pendleton would have gone any better.

The picnickers enjoyed kettles of fried fish and Dutch oven potatoes with onions. A barbershop quartet was organized out of the attendees, and they sang songs about better times and quieter women. Clementine was content to smile at the amusements of town life, all the while comparing her own fruit pies to the assortment of pastries presented to them that evening.

She had them all beat. *It must be the butter*, she thought to herself.

Once the festivities wound down, Roy Martin drove Clementine to the boarding house. He made small talk as they traveled, feeling the need to fill every ticking second with noise. "Are you ready to see your picture on the front page of the paper tomorrow?"

"I won't be on the front," Clementine said.

"Well, of course you will. All the pictures that pushy newspaper man took today—oh, little lady, of course you'll be front and center! It's not every day a gal saves the city's sheriff."

"No—I didn't go dancing with Mr. Pendleton, and he really is enamored with Saylor and her connection to the

Seattle Times. Roxy said Saylor's grandma owns that newspaper, and she comes from a long line of media moguls. Saylor's grandma herself is actually the famous columnist Charlie Blaze. Poor Helen is enamored with his work—that's where I learned what 'enamored' even means. Anyhow, Helen is in love with Saylor's grandma, only she doesn't know it's Saylor's grandma, and Hank Pendleton would like to further his career. Saylor will be on the front cover, and not Roxy or me, or even you."

Sheriff Martin was actively listening, trying to figure out the loose ends and details. "What about the bears?" he quipped, but Clementine simply shrugged.

"Well, here we are," he said, parking near the gate. He walked around to the passenger side and thanked Clementine for the great evening. "Might I take you riding sometime? We could ride patrol around the bank, if you'd get a kick out of it."

"Maybe sometime, Sheriff Martin, but not too soon. I'm savin' myself for some kind of gosh-dern wonderful."

"I-I don't understand," the lawmen sputtered.

"Me neither. Well, g'night, Sheriff. I've got silk stockings to darn, and I'm tired."

CHAPTER SEVEN

"The true republic—men, their rights and nothing more; women, their rights and nothing less."

Susan B. Anthony

Just as Clementine suspected, Saylor Sanderson Ashton made another front page of the *Anchorage Times*. Mr. Tremblay was outraged over the blight. He slapped the headline, reading out loud, "'Local Fashionista Solves Bear Problem.'"

"I almost *can't* believe it," Florence exclaimed. "Clementine rescued the sheriff, and Roxy spent the night in the same tree he was in...but Saylor gets the credit? Typical!"

Mr. Tremblay folded up the paper and said, "There are more pictures and the whole story on page four."

"Page four," Florence muttered. "That's a slap in the face."

"I'm not fussed up," Roxy declared.

"Me neither," Clementine said. "I told the sheriff that's how it would be."

The day sped by. Clementine was becoming a good hand at the switchboard. She didn't panic when folks wanted information. "I've come to terms with the facts, Helen," she said. "I either know what they want and tell them, or I admit I don't know and try to find out. There's no sense frettin' a lick over stuff one way or another."

"You're right," Helen agreed, "but don't let laziness be your excuse for not knowing things. You should try reading in the evenings."

"Golly, Helen, a person's gotta rest sometime! By the time I'm finished helping Mrs. Lawrence with dishes, I'm bushwhacked. But when I decide to read something, I try to make it a cookbook."

"I don't know the details of your rent, but helping Mrs. Lawrence is not your career. Being Information is."

"Well lucky I *do* know how to read," Clementine said defensively.

Roxy invited Clementine to go downtown after work. Roxy was hoping to go into Archer Merchandise to shop for curtain fabric. "Yes, while you're looking there, I think I might go across the street and into Ashton's. I'd like to buy a new hat—I'll call it my Thinkin' Cap so Helen won't say I'm bein' lazy in my learnin'.."

"That's using your head," Roxy said. "And by the way, I'm glad you weren't too upset about the newspaper headline."

"Gals like us, Roxy, really weren't born for the front page. I'm glad Saylor was, though, cuz she's the nicest and most generous front-pager that ever was."

The walk was pleasant, and Clementine was so happy to have made friends. Soon Roxy would become Mrs. Reese Remington, and the couple decided they would move two hundred miles south of Anchorage to Homer. "I don't reckon I know who will end up my roommate."

Roxy nodded. "I've had seven since I've been here."

"Poor Mr. Tremblay," Clementine said. She so very often

commiserated with him. "It just ain't fair—he's forever havin' to hire new operators."

Roxy laughed merrily. "Oh, it's plenty fair, Clementine. Men outnumber us seven to one in this town. Mr. Tremblay should just learn to expect the worst as soon as the training begins."

"He already did expect the worst when I showed up," Clementine said. "I'd like to think I'd be the last one of us to be unfaithful to the switchboard cause. For some reason, I just feel so deeply loyal."

"Well, I am not sorry that it is my time to flee-fly away," Roxy said. "Everyone deserves some happiness. Somehow the switchboard doesn't make me feel as good as Reese does."

Clementine snorted a very unladylike laugh. "What about the Gagnons? Do you suppose Helen and Hazel will ever meet the men of their dreams?"

"Doubtful at this point. They're in their forties."

"I got a set of twin brothers in their forties, and I might like to try havin' a pie bakin' competition sometime and invite Hardy and Heath."

"Oh, you're scheming! Saylor will be so pleased to mark her influence on you," Roxy said as the pair reached Main Street. "Okay, I'll meet you in a little while."

"Bye," Clementine called. She waited for three horse-drawn wagons, a truck, and a bicycle to go by before she dared dash across the road to Ashton's.

The doorbell chimed, and Saylor looked up from a wedding display she was working on. "Clementine, what a lovely surprise," she called.

"I had a few dollars just a burnin' a hole in my pocket,"

Clementine confessed.

"Of course. You came to the right place," Saylor cried happily. Andy smiled from his desk behind the counter.

Andy's mother also smiled at Clementine, probably remembering the countrified shipwreck she once resembled. "Miss Clark," Mrs. Ivy Ashton welcomed kindly, "you are the prettiest woman in this town!"

"No, Saylor is," Clementine said, but she was all smiles to land a compliment from the previously austere clerk. "But I don't mind a bit! Saylor's nice as pie."

"That she is," Ivy Ashton agreed.

"I'm glad you came, Clementine. I need to show you the dress I ordered, especially for you, to wear to Roxy's wedding." The bubbly blonde socialite grabbed Clementine by the hand and led her into the stockroom.

"What? I get to go to Roxy's wedding? I ain't never been to a weddin' before."

"Well, I'm in charge of this one, and so you are coming."

"I am?"

"Yes, I already invited the Tremblays and asked them to bring you."

"Well, I'll be a mule's ear!" Clementine cried. "But I only have twelve dollars cash saved up, and only brung seven with me."

"'*Brought*'. As the self-designated matron of honor, I've taken care of all the monetary details." And also, because Saylor was wealthy as any three kings. "But Clementine, you keep your attendance a secret, okay? We'll surprise Roxy."

And right there, on a hanger next to Roxy's glorious,

elegant, completely died-and-gone-to-heaven wedding gown was a white and baby-blue print crepe satin flapper-length dress. The skirt was pleated smartly, and Clementine couldn't wait to twirl in it just to see what the pleats would do. "Well, I ain't never, not in all my born life, seen such a lovely thing," she solemnly proclaimed.

"You mean you haven't ever. '*Ain't*' ain't a word."

"'*Isn't,*'" Clementine corrected, making them both giggle.

"Would you say my dove gray pumps would be the best shoes to wear with it?"

"No. Look what I did," Saylor said, nudging a shoebox toward the unsuspecting woman.

"Shoes, too?" Clementine felt her eyes dilate to the size of dinner plates. She couldn't wait to knock the lid off and examine them. "Oh, these make me shiver, they are so fantabulous!"

Clementine quickly lifted one. The shoes were white satin—perfectly matching the dress, but tiny blue flowers rimmed the ankle straps. The flowers matched the exact blue in the dress. "I'm without words," Clementine babbled. "I'm utterly confloundered!"

"'Confounded,'" Saylor corrected. "But you are a natural dresser!"

"Should I wear a hat with this *ensemble*?" Clementine heavily seasoned the word so Saylor would see she'd committed her first fashion lessons to memory.

"Yes, this one." Saylor slid a hatbox over to Clementine.

"What? Oh, I love it!" Clementine cried. It wasn't just any hat. "This is the smartest, most sophisticatedest head-topper in the world!"

"It's 'sophisticated.' Not 'sophisticatedest.'"

"You're wrong, Saylor, for once. This hat really is sophisticatedest because a regular word like 'sophisticated' isn't strong enough."

"Let's go try it all on," Saylor suggested, thrilled by Clementine's response.

A grand-style hoopla took place in the dressing room that day. And more than once, Saylor said, "You are going to sell a dozen of these dresses just by wearing this one."

Clementine was giddy at the words. "You mean I could be a walking billboard like Mr. Lawrence says you are?"

"Oh, yes," Saylor said with the most assuring manner. "And once the Gagnon sisters and Mrs. Tremblay learn you have new clothes to wear to the grand event, they too shall have to come do some shopping."

At this point, Ivy Ashton was used to Saylor's generous sales tactics. Clementine came into the store with seven dollars to spend, which she *did* spend—every cent on new shoes and a cloche—but she left the store with fifty dollars' worth of merchandise.

"No, Clementine, don't let Roxy see all that," Saylor said. "Andy and I will deliver these around later. I don't want to ruin the surprise for Roxy, and she will be so thrilled to see you at the wedding. Just take what you came in for today so she doesn't suspect a thing."

Clementine hugged the ever-generous, nearly magical Saylor. She had blown into Anchorage like a fairy godmother of sorts, casting the most beautiful spells. Clementine fully appreciated the sparkling difference she'd made in her life.

"There once was a lady with style and grace who wore a smile upon her face. Her eyes twinkled kindly; she was genuinely good…especially to those most often misunderstood."

Tears welled instantly in both Ivy and Saylor's eyes. "Why, Clementine Clark—" Saylor began.

"It's a little talent of mine, makin' things rhyme. Mr. Pendleton called it ex-temp-a-somethin' or another, but I have no idea what that means. All I know is I can rattle them right off the top of my head."

"That is *extemporaneous* indeed," Ivy agreed. "You are gifted, Miss Clark, and I agree very much with your assessment of my daughter-in-law. I could not have chosen better for Andy than he chose for himself."

Hank Pendleton came calling later that evening, even though Clementine requested he not show up so soon. "I wanted to apologize about the photo I chose for the headline."

"No need. Roxy Reynolds doesn't get fussed up over stuff, and neither do I. And I could never be jealous of Saylor because I love her too much."

"Well, if she was the one who coordinated you, as you say, we are all in her debt," the reporter said as they took a turn around the lawn. "I'd love to take you to dinner one evening this weekend. Would you let me know when you are available?"

"I ain't available at all because I'm promised to my brothers this weekend. I'd better visit once in a while so they don't forget me."

"Maybe another time, then? It's for certain I won't forget you." The man seemed quite earnest, but Clementine pegged him to be very attentive to all the women he knew.

When the weekend came, Sheriff Roy Martin was happy to give her a ride. "Have you thought any more about the security at the bank?" Clementine asked by way of conversation.

"You needn't worry your pretty head about that," he said, convincing her she would run for sheriff when his bid was up.

"Thank you for the ride," she said, not even waiting for him to come around to her side and open the door.

"Aren't you even going to invite me in?" he asked, seeming very disappointed.

"Better not. My brothers shoot almost as well as I do." Clementine laughed innocently, adding, "I'm not sure they've kept house without me."

"I see, honey, I see. Well, I'll swing by Sunday evening and give you a ride back to town, if you'd like."

"About what time?" Clementine asked.

"What time's best?"

"About eight o'clock, unless that's past your bedtime."

"I'll be here," he called, thinking perhaps he was winning with her.

Clementine dodged into the cabin, loving the feeling of being home. Tears pricked her eyes as she peered around, seeing that her brothers had been trying hard to keep things neat. "They do need wives." She quickly began mixing biscuits for supper, knowing this would be a real surprise for them.

Clementine measured, sifted, and baked. The cabin began advertising the tempting aromas. Surely the smell would call her brothers home from the mill! She stirred milk gravy in a cast-iron skillet, using bacon grease for flavor. She set the table, finding berry preserves from the previous year in the pantry.

"Li'l Sis is home," Heath cried, nearly taking the door off its hinges.

Clementine jumped up and down excitedly. In her head, she was twelve years old again, but Pete said, "You've turned into such a female, I can't hardly believe you're my sister!"

"She was born a female, you dunce," Hardy said. "We're the dumb bunch that nearly train-wrecked her charm."

Dressing smartly was becoming second nature to Clementine, and she'd enlarged her inventory of nice clothes and accessories little by little. "Thank you," she replied, happy to know that even brothers could notice.

The men washed up and took their places around the table. Clementine set a basket of biscuits in the center, and a bowl full of gravy with a ladle. "Biscuits and gravy," she said, "since there wasn't no meat in the icebox."

"You ain't been here to kill some," Matthew drawled comically.

"We've missed ya," Hardy agreed with a wink.

"Well, I killed some bacon grease so you won't even miss eatin' meat tonight. And once you're done with biscuits and gravy, you can load up on biscuits and jam."

While the siblings ate, Clementine entertained them with tales of town—of switchboard life and all its rigors. She regaled her heroic deeds in saving the sheriff, and how he was sweet on her.

"I don't feel the same way back, but I've become a scheming sort of gal since I let him drive me around where I really need to go."

"This is why dames scare me spitless," Matthew said. "I ain't got no car."

"I'm figurin' on runnin' for sheriff," Clementine mentioned. "Then I'd have a truck and deputies to do my biddin'. I figure I could learn how to drive."

Pete smiled at his baby sister across the table. "Runnin' for sheriff? *You*?"

And then he guffawed and hurrahed and made such a fuss that Clementine finally told him to stop. "Pete, I'm not teasin'."

"You mean you *ain't* teasin'," Matthew corrected.

"Pipe down," Heath growled. "Li'l Sis can be the sheriff if she wants to be! I'd vote for her."

"Better rethink it, Li'l Sis," Hardy said. He made a swirling motion around the chest area and said, "Your badge wouldn't hang straight." Then all the brothers laughed again, but they didn't mean no harm, and to prove it, they invited Clementine to do the milkin' and to tend Hilde and the chickens.

"I don't mind," Clementine answered brightly. "I've missed everything around here." She accidentally pronounced the g. It was gradually happening more and more.

"Enough to quit and come home?" Heath quizzed hopefully.

"Naw. I'm makin' a real career for myself. I like having a little money, and I like dressing well."

"Dressing?" Matthew quizzed again, not liking the

influence the grammar patrol was havin' on his sister.

"Believe it or not, I'm makin' progress in speaking," Clementine bragged. She put on Pete's old boots and grabbed the milk bucket. "When I'm done with chores, I'm challengin' Pete to an Indian leg wrestle. None of the ladies will wrestle me—and I think I could whip all but Florence, maybe."

"How tough is this Florence?" Matthew asked.

"She's the self-proclaimed boss of the Switchboard Sisterhood, and just a little thick in the thigh."

CHAPTER EIGHT

"It is such a happiness when two good people get together—and they always do."

Jane Austen

Clementine's first ferry ride was exciting. She, the Tremblays, and the Gagnon twins were the only ones able to attend Roxy Reynolds' wedding. "Someone has to cover the boards," Florence said, and she stepped up to the task like a champ. Still, Clementine found it interesting that Saylor had chosen her to attend and not one of the other, more refined, ladies.

However, next to Saylor, Clementine figured she might have been Roxy's best roommate and second-best friend. The two of them had never fussed up over nothin', and Clementine wasn't offended. Why, before moving into Anchorage, Clementine had only been friends with Hilde, old Floss and Blossom, the hens, her brothers, and herself.

"I always did love me," she admitted, hanging over the front rail, catching a bit of reflection. With her new hat, the dress, and the shoes, she felt as fancy as a seven-layer cake with dollops of buttercream and carefully piped florets. "How do you do?" she practiced to herself, summoning all she'd learned about etiquette. Perhaps it was the clothes. "I am a wedding guest of honor. I was coordinated at Ashton's Women's Shop, and I don't mind being a walking billboard. Not one little bitty bit."

"Don't let the wind steal your hat," Helen advised. She wasn't the most daring of Clemetine's acquaintances. Helen preferred to read about adventures rather than actually having them, and in her hand at that very moment was a copy of Jane Austen's *Emma*.

"My mother liked that book," Clementine said, surprising all who knew her. "I read it too, but it wasn't my favorite until just this very minute, as I realize that crazy Saylor *is* Emma Woodhouse." She exchanged smiles with Julie Tremblay. Hazel wasn't actually listening to Clementine, because she seldom did, but Helen scowled slightly, as if considering the very truth of the statement.

During the journey, Mr. Tremblay spotted several orcas. Clementine had never seen whales before, and it gave her a thrill. "There once was an ocean deep, with secrets she just couldn't keep—like big arching whales, and their wonderful tales. Oh, how I love watching them leap!"

Mrs. Tremblay was astonished, exclaiming, "You are quite a poet, Miss Clark. I would never have guessed."

"That makes two of us," Helen replied. Boy, was this a day of surprises!

Clementine couldn't take her eyes off the vistas. She tried scanning the water for more whales. She did spot a big grizzly walking along a shoreline, but he was at a distance, making him a little bear. Clementine smiled at the thought.

"I hope there's dancing at the wedding," Hazel said, joining Clementine at the ferry's bow.

"Well, who would you dance with if there is? There's not likely to be any eligible bachelors."

"I'll settle for Helen, then. I've made her dance with me before." The women laughed. "Oh, see the colorful little dots in the distance, Clementine? They are houses in Homer. Roxy's house is one of the stilted ones."

And it suddenly all seemed romantic. Clementine hadn't given love much thought. The world was so big and so large, she'd mostly just gotten by from day to day—but these new experiences were turning her heart toward something more magnificent than Indian leg wrestling and homemade butter. She sighed wistfully, homesick for things and people she'd never yet met. It's for sure she didn't love Sheriff Martin or Hank Pendleton, either one. They didn't even stir her heart the way the orcas had.

The small church in Homer was decorated beautifully to match the occasion. Mrs. Tremblay pointed out the finer details to Clementine. "I cannot believe this is your first wedding," she said a time or two.

"Well, believe it," Clementine said. "I hope it won't be my last."

"With the marriage service I'm running?" Mr. Tremblay asked sarcastically. "Surely you jest!"

"I'm loyal to ya," Clementine said sympathetically.

Reese Remington took his place at the front of the chapel. He was handsome. It had shocked everyone in the Lawrence Boarding House when he first came calling. Roxy had been healing from a tragic heartbreak, and suddenly this horseback-riding outdoors reporter was on the scene. It had been a whirlwind romance—Roxy fell hard and fast, and so, apparently, did he.

The music started, and the guests rose to their feet. Roxy's English students came in first, scattering rose petals along the way. Then came Saylor, decked to the nines, and then Roxy started up the aisle on her widowed mother's arm. Saylor had pulled off a miracle getting the practical woman out of Wyoming.

Roxy was an elegant bride, and the intense expression on Mr. Remington's face as she glided up the aisle was beyond compare. He loved her! Oh, how that love was evident, and something deep and yearning sprouted inside Clementine. She wanted to feel as head over heels as they were. That was the "some kind of wonderful" she was looking for.

Clementine peeked sideways. Poor Mr. Tremblay! He had no idea that in the last twenty-one seconds, her heart had become engaged. To whom, however, she hadn't a clue.

The newlyweds, Reese and Roxy, didn't stay too long at the party after the ceremony. Saylor's shindig went on without them. The honored guests grazed on a variety of fruit tarts, pastries, wedding cake, and ice cream. Clementine visited with Saylor just long enough to tell her she wanted to have a pie-baking competition. Excitement for a new project flashed in Saylor's eyes. Clementine sighed happily because Saylor knew how to organize these types of affairs, and she did not.

"If I can't talk the mayor into a fall social complete with a pie-baking contest, I shall sponsor it myself," Saylor said with an affirmative nod. Blonde curls bounced with the motion.

Andy and Saylor danced. The Tremblays danced. Helen and Hazel danced. Hazel eventually dragged Clementine onto her feet. "I know you don't know how to dance, so I'm going to show you!" And she did. It wasn't scary dancing with Hazel, and nobody cared that Clementine was just learning.

All too soon, however, Mr. Tremblay announced it was time to return to the ferry. It was, unfortunately, a five-hour journey back to Anchorage.

"I can teach you more dances on the boat," Hazel said.

"You two are apt to embarrass me," Helen hissed, but Hazel didn't let her sister's protest dissuade her one bit.

Clementine was pleased. Out of the Gagnon twins, it had only been Helen who had been attentive to her. Now, however, it seemed Hazel was extending her friendship as well, and in a fun and exciting way! Since Clementine had decided to become engaged sooner rather than later, learning to dance had suddenly become her duty. Poor Mr. Tremblay, indeed.

The trip home was fun. Most people went inside the ferry and slept, but Hazel and Clementine danced on the deck beneath the moon and the stars. Clementine learned to waltz, to dance the turkey trot, and best of all, the Charleston. "I never thought I could learn this stuff," Clementine admitted.

"I love dancing. I go at least twice a week while Helen stays home and reads three more books."

"I also enjoy reading, but I like baking and other things, too."

Hazel said, "And while dressed to the hilt, you also say g's on the end of your words. You've spoken well all day."

"Shucks, I ain't had nothin' better to do," Clementine teased. "Do you think that's what the whales were doing earlier? Were they dancing? Just because it's fun?"

"I never considered such a thing, but perhaps that's exactly what they were doing. I doubt they call it the turkey trot, though."

Clementine laughed. "Nothing can top this day! My first time away from home, my first wedding, my first dancing."

"You'll enjoy it more with a man," Hazel promised. "I also prefer it that way, especially if they're not drunk."

"You're a good dance teacher. Have you considered giving lessons?"

"I haven't," Hazel said, considering it now, possibly for the first time.

"Well, it's just that I've got me four brothers, and not one of them can dance."

"Brothers? *Four?* Are they handsome?"

"Yes, but they don't speak any better than I do."

"Conversation isn't everything," Hazel said. "Did you notice the look on Mr. Remington's face today as Roxy marched up the aisle? No words were necessary to say exactly what needed to be said."

"Yes, I picked up on that. I felt ready to become engaged myself, but I'm not gonna say nothin' to Mr. Tremblay about it."

"Are you serious with someone?" Hazel quizzed.

"Not yet, but I'm serious about getting that way after I *do* meet a good one."

Hazel tittered. "Oh, how I wish that approach had worked for me. Blessedly, we are living in modern times, and if a man doesn't ever turn up, I can claim I had a career!"

"Wait till you meet Heath...or Hardy, take your pick. They're twins. Or Matthew or Pete, but Pete's probably too young."

"Yes, I have no intention of raising a half-raised man."

"Oh, he's raised, but he's thirty-two. Hardy and Heath are forty-two."

"Ten years of life experience is important," Hazel said, honestly giving Clementine's brothers serious thought.

"I think Heath looks just like Pa, and I thought Pa was handsome."

"What about Hardy?"

"He looks just like Heath," Clementine said.

Hazel laughed. "You are a funny thing."

"Well, Saylor is going to plan a shindig in Anchorage. There will be a pie-baking contest, dancing, a trap shoot, Indian leg wrestles—things like that. Maybe that would be a great time to invite them to town." Clementine would now need to plant dancing, wrestling, and trap shoots into Saylor's scheming mind.

"Sounds vulgar. Sign me up," Hazel quipped humorously. "It's not too good for Anchorage, though. We are the rough Alaskan sort."

"Except for Helen," Clementine said.

"That's right. All except for Helen."

CHAPTER NINE

"It was a beautiful, bright autumn day, with air like cider and a sky so blue you could drown in it."

Diana Gabaldon

Three weeks later, Saylor came through with Clementine's much-anticipated Anchorage Fall Festival. There was a contest for the best pie in three categories—cream pies, fruit pies, and savory pies. There would be apple bobbing, pumpkin carving, gunnysack and three-legged races for the kids, then Indian leg wrestles, trap shooting, and dancing until midnight.

Clementine had tried to teach her brothers all that Hazel had taught her about dancing. "I promise, fellas, it's fun! It's time you clean up and go to town for sociable reasons."

"I ain't never been sociable," Pete whined as if he were six.

"Ya mean ya ain't never been clean," Matthew teased.

While they polished their boots and oiled the harnesses fit for town, Clementine baked her heart out. She planned on entering every category. She had all the fresh butter and cream a pastry chef could want. "I'm makin' Ma's harvest berry pie."

"I hope I get to be the judge," Heath said, remembering Ma's perfect crust and the way she simmered apples, blackberries, strawberries, and rhubarb together with the right amount of sugar and just a naughty little splash of rum.

"What kind of cream pie are ya makin', Li'l Sis?" Pete asked.

"I'm going to make an old-fashioned brown sugar custard pie, with maple whipped cream so stiff it could salute the flag."

"I hope I'm a dad-blame judge too!"

"Well, you won't be. Saylor's already selected the judges."

"Sounds fishy," Pete grumbled.

"And I'm makin' rabbit pie for my savory entry."

Pete asked, "How does a person qualify to be a judge?"

"Saylor asked the owner of Moose Tracks Bakery, Mayor Beasley, and Mrs. Kennedy. She's the waitress at the Frisco Café, and she bakes all their pies."

"How does a guy become mayor?" Pete persisted, wishing to qualify as a judge.

"It's an elected position, Pete. You're disqualified already on account of livin' outside the city limits."

"What a stuck-up rule," Pete complained, "holdin' a man's address again' him."

"I'm gonna run for sheriff if I'm not engaged by the next election," Clementine promised.

The brothers laughed again, thinking their little sister was a real comedian.

Soon the cabin smelled of such tantalizing aromas, Clementine baked three extra pies just for her brothers to eat. She couldn't bear the whining—and to be honest, they did smell and look delicious. She was grateful her day off had come before the festival so she could get ready. She couldn't bake the pies at the boarding house because Ethel Lawrence was entering the competition too.

"Of course, Mrs. Lawrence consistently makes good pie. She baked a lemon meringue pie just for me after I saved the sheriff, and also to thank me for milkin' Contessa on occasion. But Contessa don't give the sweetest cream, so the butter's not as good as what we get from old Floss and Blossom. I hope she don't raise my rent when I beat her out of all three categories."

Being the best older brothers in the world, they listened and encouraged, and snarfed up the pie like four greedy pigs. "Golly, fellas. I really do wish you *was* the judges."

It was the crispest Saturday of October. Clementine did the barnyard chores, then changed into her fun plaid dress. It was just the perfect occasion for red shoes. Heath brought the wagon around. Clementine's pies were packed smartly so they wouldn't get joggled en route. Pa's rifle was in a scabbard because Clementine planned on winning the trap shoot too. "I'm bound to get one of two things after today, fellas."

"What's that?" Hardy asked.

"Engaged or elected."

"Hopefully you don't outshoot the man who wished to woo you," Heath remarked smartly.

"I do feel terribly bad for Mr. Tremblay. Before Roxy's wedding, I was satisfied with my switchboard career, and nothin' could have dragged me away, but seein' the way Mr. Remington looked at her while she marched up the aisle was somethin' else again! I can't shake wantin' that for myself now."

"Poor Sheriff Martin is more like it," Matthew added. "He's either loosin' his gal or his job."

"I ain't his gal," Clementine objected.

"You let him drive you all over tarnation," Pete said. "But you claim you ain't his gal." He shook his head. "Women terrify me. I might be sorry I got all slicked up for this shindig."

Thirty pies loomed before the judges. The first category they judged was cream pies. Clementine felt hopeful because the owner of Moose Tracks Bakery ate his entire slice of old-fashioned brown sugar custard, and Mrs. Kennedy pushed her spoon against a pillar of whipped cream, impressed by the look and texture. She would take a bite, then smack her lips, trying to discern the exact ingredients.

Mrs. Lawrence scowled when they lifted the brown sugar custard pie high in the air and said, "This is the winner!"

Next to be judged were the fruit pies. Mrs. Lawrence was confident in her blueberry. Indeed, the color was deep, and the berries looked enticing as Mrs. Kennedy cut a slice. It was a definite contender! But Clementine was certain about Ma's harvest berry pie. Mayor Beasley licked his lips and angled his head after the first nibble. He went in for a hungry second bite while spectators smiled.

Only the participants knew which pies were theirs. Heath leaned down and whispered, "The look on his face says it all."

The mayor finished the second bite, saying, "My, my,

my! Such pie, pie, pie!"

Mrs. Kennedy took her dainty bites, trying to decipher what exactly made it taste so good. "It's the rum," Hardy whispered.

With a unanimous decision, they lifted the harvest berry pie in the air. The Clark brothers cheered and whistled. Mrs. Lawrence's chin quivered dejectedly. Then a small recess was taken so the judges could walk off all that starch.

Mrs. Kennedy leaned close to Clementine and said, "Honey, you could write cookbooks!"

"Really?" Clementine quizzed gleefully, "Me? You're too kind, but I do thank you!"

A few gunny sack races were won in the interim, and then the pie judging resumed in earnest. Mrs. Kennedy was careful to cut smaller slices. "I'm about ready to pop already," she said, drawing laughter from all around.

Mrs. Lawrence had prepared a turkey pie full of dark meat and veggies from her garden. There were chicken pies, beef pies, and even a venison pie, but Clementine's was the only rabbit pie, and she'd roasted the meat to velvet. It had to win, Heath said, because nobody in the world could make richer gravy than Li'l Sis.

"This crust is something," Mayor Beasley confessed.

The baker agreed. "And that rich stew inside is so flavorful!"

Mrs. Kennedy nibbled, then took a bite, then a bigger bite, forgetting how full she was. This dish needed to be on menus everywhere. "This baker put a bit of rosemary in that buttery crust—can you taste that?"

The baker took another bite, nibbling slowly. His face lit

up and he said, "If I'm not mistaken, this person made rosemary butter."

Mrs. Kennedy nodded her head, smiling. "It's a subtle infusion, and it works perfectly with the rabbit."

Saylor flashed a smile in Clementine's direction and held up both hands to show she was crossing her fingers for her friend. Mayor Beasley made the announcement. "And the winner, winner, winner of this entry is the rabbit pie. It's good, good, good!"

Mrs. Lawrence fought back tears. Mr. Lawrence was quick to lend her his handkerchief. Clementine was suddenly sorry she'd swept the contest—even though it had been her dream. "I'd like to dedicate my victory to Mrs. Ethel Lawrence," Clementine called. The crowd quieted. "She is consistently better in every way. I just got lucky today."

"There's no luck to it," Mrs. Kennedy said. "And it was blind judging. We couldn't have known all three pies were yours."

"Thank you, Mrs. Lawrence," Clementine said again.

It cushioned Mrs. Lawrence's pride a little bit, and Clementine was far too useful at the boarding house to be angry with her. Mr. Lawrence, however, had this to say. "That's a poor way to treat your teacher! Ethel has welcomed you into her kitchen, and you repay her like this? What are you, a little pirate?"

"My mother's recipe cards taught me to cook. Pa taught me to read them. They're both proud today—I've pirated nothing!" Clementine retorted, and she was done trying to soothe second-place winners and various other losers.

"Hey, doll, let's get a picture for the paper," a familiar voice said.

"Hi, Mr. Pendleton," Clementine called, as if she'd never strolled around the yard with him before. "Let me see if I can find Saylor. You'll want *her* for sure."

"Ouch," the reporter said, gripping his heart. "I thought you said you didn't get fussed up over stuff."

"I don't," Clementine responded. "Oh, Saylor, come here! Mr. Pendleton wants your picture for the paper!"

"Come on, Clementine, don't be like this!" Hank said. "I don't need her in your picture—not this time."

"Well, you certainly do!" Clementine replied. "This whole festival was her idea! Now you have smiles to give and pictures to take—and it takes a real headliner for that." The barb was intended to jab and sting, but Clementine's voice sugar-coated every syllable so one could hardly call her mean.

"At least save a dance for me tonight!"

Clementine nodded and waved goodbye without turning. She had things to shoot now that the pies were taken care of. Just to make things nice and fun, Saylor asked Sheriff Martin and his deputies to participate in the shooting event. Clementine relished the idea of blasting Ducky Puddles right out of the water. By now, most of the folks at the park knew who Clementine Clark was. She was a pie-making son of a gun, and they naturally followed her across the grass.

"Hey there, little lady," the lawman called. He was head over *red* high heels in love with her. By using the affectionate term, he meant to scare other men away, but in reality, the sticky words loaded Clementine's gun.

Clementine leaned close to the sheriff and whispered, "There are plans in the works to rob the bank tonight. You'd better station some deputies over there to keep watch."

Sheriff Martin grinned, murmuring, "Don't worry your sweet head about a thing."

"That's on you, then," Clementine replied.

One deputy, who was also president of the Anchorage Gun Club, barked, "No women allowed in this competition."

"Why not?" Clementine challenged. "Men got to enter pies. Why can't women shoot?"

"Because it's just not how it's done," he answered indignantly.

"Well, sonny, welcome to the new age," Clementine countered, and everyone laughed.

Andy Ashton spoke up then. "What are you afraid of, Larry?"

"Certainly not her," the deputy said.

"Then let her shoot," Andy pressed. "And for heaven's sake, show some manners!"

The deputy apologized. "I'm sorry, Miss . . .?"

"Clark," Clementine repeated as if he didn't know his boss was sweet on her.

Forty men entered the competition, and only one Clementine. It took all afternoon, but eventually every man was eliminated, leaving only one woman in a fun plaid number to collect the trophy. Sheriff Roy Martin was a sore loser until all the other men were likewise humiliated. Then he began touting his lady as Annie Oakley reincarnate.

"I don't recall Clementine belongin' to anyone," Heath said, stepping in front of the lawman. "But Li'l Sis has whooped this day to bits! You fellas better see if you can bob for apples better than you can shoot. Shucks, there ain't no man in this town that deserves my sister!"

"Heath, leave him alone," Clementine said. "I can fight my own battles."

Heath grunted something and the sheriff grunted something else, and that was the end of that.

"Boy, oh boy, it's been your day," Hank Pendleton called. "I really do need a picture of you with your gun. I'm seeing the headline now. *Pie Baking Champ Shoots the Clouds Out of the Sky*!"

Clementine smiled and nodded. "Just a minute then, Hank." Then she put her hands up to her mouth and blasted, "Hey, Saylor! Get over here! This reporter needs your picture for the newspaper again!"

The spectators laughed. This previously unknown woman was getting some pretty good licks in today. Hank Pendleton took his comeuppance well, but whatever pictures he took of Clementine that day were probably ones of her walking away.

CHAPTER TEN

"I ain't afraid to love a man. I ain't afraid to shoot him either."

Annie Oakley

Clementine rode to Ashton's with Saylor so they could change outfits for the dance. They giggled the whole way at what a success Saylor's grand event had been and how Clementine Clark had introduced herself to the town.

"Wait till they see your dress for the dance," Saylor said.

Clementine giggled. Oh, how their plans had blossomed over the past three weeks. "I got a job offer from the Frisco Café, and one from Moose Tracks Bakery."

"And twenty-nine wedding proposals," Saylor added.

"No *serious* offers however."

"You wait till the dance, Clementine! You just wait."

Saylor unlocked the back door of the shop, and Clementine followed her upstairs to Saylor and Andy's apartment. It was so cozy and inviting! "I love your place," she said. "Hopefully someday I can become engaged and have happy homes like you and Roxy."

"Speaking of Roxy," Saylor said, "I talk to her on the phone weekly, and she's doing well! She and Reese are madly in love, and her widowed mother—do you remember meeting her?"

"Yes," Clementine said. "She was just as brunette and lovely as her daughter."

"Well, Mrs. Reynolds is engaged to marry Mr. Justice Vance!"

"I don't remember Mr. Vance—"

"He's the very nice man who sold Reese and Roxy the house—and he's basically putting Homer on the map."

"Is he the mayor?"

"He's a dreamer and schemer like us," Saylor said, showing Clementine into a guest room.

"I'm not a schemer," Clementine insisted, eyes wide open and innocent. Then she saw the prettiest, most daring dress hanging on the wardrobe.

"For me?"

"That is the dress of a champion," Saylor said. "Hurry into it—we don't want to miss a thing! There's a mirror behind the door."

Clementine couldn't believe it. She was modern, all right. She'd never before shown her shoulders, but this sequin-detailed dress was sleeveless. and the skirt boasted twelve-inch flirtatious fringe! She felt like Hazel had when she'd said "Sounds vulgar. Count me in!" The dress fit her like a glove. "Oh, I can't wait to spin in you," Clementine said, pirouetting around the room just to feel the fringe fly around her knees. She then slid her feet into enviable Mary Janes that were attractive enough to dance on their own power.

"Do you love it?" Saylor called through the door.

"Yes, and I love you, too! This is perfect!" She walked into the living room with a big smile.

"Holy smokes, Clementine. You're the queen of the day!" Saylor applied bright red lipstick to her friend's lips, then crowned her with a jeweled headband. "Now you're positively...sexy!"

Clementine gasped at the use of such a wanton, wicked word. Saylor giggled and said, "I am *never* allowed to use that word in the shop. It would make my mother-in-law's proper head explode, but to my dear friend, I may be so bold."

Saylor guided Clementine back to the mirror. Clementine gasped again because Saylor was right. She *was* sexy. "What will Mr. Tremblay think me of now?"

"That you'll become engaged."

"I hope he doesn't think I *have* to..."

"It doesn't so much matter what Mr. Tremblay thinks—I think he enjoys his daily headaches." Saylor dropped the lipstick tube into Clementine's matching clutch. "Keep this for touchups."

"The sisterhood, misunderstood, is up to no good in the neighborhood," Clementine rhymed to Saylor's delight. The women went down the steps and out the back door.

"And here we are, back in the car," Saylor continued wittily.

"Back to the park before it gets dark," Clementine added. "We must hurry and scurry before my brothers worry!"

Saylor parked, and the women exited the car. There was that pesky reporter, camera on the tripod, and poof! He captured the ladies just as they'd linked arms. "That is what I call a pair of dolls," he said.

"I'm sure you're clever enough to edit me out," Clementine called without breaking stride.

Saylor tittered merrily, and they continued toward the pavilion where the catcalls and whistles made wives bristle.

Mayor Beasley announced, "Now ladies and gentlemen, before we dance, dance, dance, you must fill out your cards, cards, cards. This is a fun social and should include every, every, everyone!"

Suddenly Hazel was there, standing near Clementine. "What did I miss? Everything? I didn't think Mr. Tremblay would *ever* let us punch out."

"No, Hazel, the dance hasn't started yet—and look, there are my brothers." Clementine tugged the redhead by the hand. "Hey, Hardy and Heath, I'd like you to meet my supervisor, Hazel Gagnon."

Hardy blushed, and Heath smiled. "Are you the one that taught Li'l Sis how to dance?"

"Guilty," Hazel said with a smile. Goodness, she certainly wasn't shy.

"I don't know how these cards work," Heath said with a shrug.

"They work like this," Hazel said. She grabbed a pen from behind her ear and signed Hazel Gagnon on the top line.

Heath was stunned, Clementine was shocked, and Hardy—well, he was plum out of luck.

"Holy buckets," Matthew said, blinking his eyes as Hazel hooked her arm through Heath's and led him onto the dance floor.

"She's a career girl," Clementine explained. "Hazel and her twin sister, Helen, have been with the Spruce Telephone Company since its inception. They know everything there is to know about makin' connections."

"I guess so," Pete said humorously.

Vivian, Nora, and Tracy must have ridden with Hazel. Fellas started buzzin' just as soon as they reached the pavilion. Florence stood nearby, waiting and waiting for her dumb beau, Joe, to sign her card. Clementine motioned her over. "I'd like you to meet Matthew, Pete, and Hardy. They're my brothers."

Florence said "Nice to meet you" so demurely that Clementine feared she was ailing. There wasn't a demure bone in Florence's whole body! Saylor said she was the self-appointed boss of the free world. That's probably why Joe, her beau, had never made a move. He was afraid of losing his agency.

Matthew seemed interested in Florence. "Ma'am, might you write your name on my card?"

"I'd be delighted," Florence said.

Come to think of it, Matthew could use a good boss. Clementine chuckled as Florence set out to conquer his two left feet.

Joe didn't yet realize his date was otherwise employed. He was busy smoking with some of his buddies. One of them, a man Clementine had never seen before, was drinking from a flask in his pocket. Prohibition never ended anyone's habits—it simply made it a sport to conceal them. If Clementine had been sheriff, she'd have clapped the man in handcuffs and made an example of him.

Instead, she caught the stranger's eye, and he asked her to sign his card. She did, dead last, and handed it back to him. "What's your name?" she asked.

"Elroy." He smiled, revealing a fat chaw tucked in his

bottom lip. What could be more enticing?

It was Clementine's duty to see that one or the other of them was passed out drunk before the last dance could come around.

Andy and Saylor danced. They were crowd pleasing, and folks made a wide circle around them. No wonder the town loved her! She was fresh and fun. Off in the shadows, Hazel taught Heath the particulars of the Charleston. He seemed to be enjoying it.

Florence danced with Matthew. Joe drank with Elroy. Clementine danced with Sheriff Martin and Hank Pendleton. She danced with the stuffy banker, Hal Hoskins, making Mrs. Hoskins glare suspiciously. She danced with a lumberjack named Hollis, and they discussed the timber business in detail. She danced with three men from the shooting competition. One of them had a familiar voice. His name was Ely Jacks.

Clementine had recently connected his call to a certain Roscoe Ellingsford of Seward. She'd accidentally overheard part of the conversation before she could disconnect herself. "We'll hit the bank on the twenty-fifth, but only if Hoskins and the sheriff are still at the fall festival. The flyer says they're to direct the trap shoot, so they'll probably stay for the dance and make sure it stays a family affair."

The switchboard operator played dumb, but she watched the man while they danced. His eyes darted around the pavilion, likely counting each deputy. Hal Hoskins was impossible to miss, as the lantern light glinted off his diamond stickpin and fat ruby ring.

Then Clementine noticed him signal, with the slightest nod of his head, toward a man who'd been content to watch Andy and Saylor. He leaned against a pavilion post, smoking a cigarette. Clementine knew of a surety that he was Roscoe Ellingsford because he'd signed her dance card.

And wheels were spinning inside Clementine's pretty head. She wasn't dumb. She was never dumb—even though she used words like "continuatin'" and "confloundered." She smiled pleasantly, and when the dance was over, she exclaimed, "Golly, guess I'd better go find Mr. Pendleton again."

Hank was ready, standing off in the shadows. "Got your camera and my scabbard?"

"Got 'em." The reporter grabbed her by the hand and led her to his car. He helped her in, and they drove down to Second Street. "You're sure about this?" Hank asked.

"Yes, Main Street is too well lit." Clementine knew the robbers wouldn't go through the front door.

"I mean, you're sure you told the sheriff?"

"At least six times this very afternoon!" Thanks for listenin' to me, Mr. Pendleton."

"It always is a pleasure."

"Oh, you typewriter types," Clementine teased. "This doesn't change anything with us, right?"

"But it'll make one stinging headline, and doll, you're the bee's knees."

The orchestra's music carried over a few blocks from the park. The robbers' plan was a good one, as nobody was apt to hear them break into the bank, and Sheriff Martin and all his deputies were dancing and eating pie.

Hank set his camera up, and Clementine situated herself on top of a nearby building. About three minutes later, Ely Jacks and Roscoe Ellingsford slinked through the back lot of the bank, and right up to the door. Jacks held a pistol while the other blew the lock with what looked like an M-80 firecracker, but it was hard to tell from Clementine's vantage point. There was a small spark and a crack, then the door opened.

"Ducky Puddles wouldn't listen to me," Clementine whispered to herself. The men disappeared inside. It took fifteen minutes for them to come out again. They each carried two bags full of money. Some of it belonged to the Spruce Telephone Company, and Clementine wasn't havin' it! She shot the bags right out of Roscoe's hands before Hank Pendleton's camera went poof beneath a curtain.

Clementine yelled, "Put your hands up! I've got you dead to rights."

Ely Jacks went for his gun, but the determined switchboard operator blew it out of his hand. The contact stung Jacks' palm and he yelped out a few cuss words. Ellingsford gathered up the money bags and took off, but he was tackled by Pete Clark. Hardy dashed out of the shadows, restraining Ely Jacks by tying his hands behind his back. Clementine climbed down and called, "I'll pose for ya now, Mr. Pendleton."

Pete dragged Ellingsford into position, and the reporter moved his camera forward and got a pretty good picture of the blonde holding a gun over both criminals. She marched Ellingsford and Jacks back to the park. It caused quite a stir, and the orchestra stopped playing completely when Clementine presented her prisoners before Sheriff Martin. "They robbed the bank. I shot the bags of cash out of their hands, Mr. Hoskins, so it should all be accounted for."

Sheriff Martin tugged at his collar, bellowing, "You should have alerted me!"

"I have, many times, asked about the security on the bank,

and this afternoon I reported the facts to you repeatedly. You kept telling me not to worry my pretty head, but all these fellas had to do to get in was blow the back lock."

"Give the money to Hoskins there," Clementine instructed her brothers. Hardy and Pete did as they were told.

Women gasped and children darted excitedly. Someone had tried robbing the bank! Mr. Hoskins stumped around, swinging his elegant walking stick while Mrs. Hoskins enjoyed a case of the vapors. Smelling salts were summoned by the mayor's wife, Liza Jane Beasley, who was only too pleased to revive her friend amid such scandal! The deputies leaped into action, and the sheriff was as wide-eyed as he could be.

"What is this town coming to?" Mrs. Hoskins squealed, as if the place had been as squeaky clean as Boise, Idaho.

The mayor stuttered, "The bank, bank, bank!"

The Clark brothers cheered, and Clementine reveled in the attention. This would help her win the election for sure! "It's lucky I don't get fussed up over much," she said to Jacks and Ellingsford as the deputies dragged them toward the sheriff's truck, "or I might've challenged you to an Indian leg wrestle. Nobody steals Mr. Tremblay's money and gets away with it!"

"And nobody can beat Li'l Sis in an Indian leg wrestle," Pete hollered. There were, however, fifteen ready volunteers.

At that point, the band played on. The Hoskins' left to go secure the bank, and they took Mayor Beasley and the Justice of the Peace, Clay Moore, along for the ride.

Saylor announced that refreshments were served. The community would have a chance to eat all the pie from the morning's pie baking competition. "But first, I'd like to thank Clementine Clark for saving our bank *and* our accounts! I hereby propose, in the stead of Mayor Beasley, to make October twenty-fifth into Clementine Clark Day!"

"Or Pie Day," Mrs. Kennedy called, taking another slice of brown sugar custard. "I've never tasted better in all my born put-together."

Everyone cheered.

CHAPTER ELEVEN

"I like to feel blonde all over."

Marilyn Monroe

The front page of the *Anchorage Times* was a doozy! There was Clementine, posing over two thugs in her sexy fringe dress with Pa's shotgun in her hands. It was a strong pose. The headline read, *Switchboard Operator, Clementine Clark, Foils Robbery.*

"'The citizens of Anchorage owe a great deal to the fringed and fearless flapper,'" Mr. Tremblay read. The sisterhood was gathered around his desk on Monday morning, getting a kick out of Clementine's many conquests. "And then here on page two, there's a picture of Clementine's winning pies. My goodness, I'm surprised Pendleton didn't include the recipes."

The ladies laughed. Florence said, "I wager he's apologizing for not having put her face on the front page after she saved the sheriff from the bears. Plus, everyone knows he's sweet on her."

"They do?" Clementine asked. "Everyone?" Gracious, that could hinder her chances of becoming engaged.

Mr. Tremblay chuckled. "On page three, there's a picture of Clementine shooting skeet. Hmm, says here, 'The confident winner of the pie baking contest went on to beat forty men in the trap shoot event. When asked why she was so proficient with a gun, she shrugged a shoulder and said, "I never learned to play with dolls.'"

Mr. Tremblay laid the paper on his desk, chuckling. "Well, Miss Clark, you managed to snag the first three pages. Of course, there is a nice big picture of Saylor on page four, wherein she is recognized for organizing such a well-attended event."

"Praises," Florence grumbled. "She'll be the governor before Alaska gets statehood."

"That's not a bad idea," Hazel chirped.

"Saylor is running for governor?" Clementine asked, eyes wide. "And she never said a word about it!"

"Don't you know I'm sarcastic?" Florence asked flatly.

Clementine's brows shot high, making her eyes larger still. "Really? I just thought you were American!" She couldn't wait to tell Matthew about *this*.

Everyone laughed themselves into hysteria at that—Mr. Tremblay included.

"Oh, blondie," Florence gasped. "You foiled the bank robbery and swept the competitions on Saturday, but you honestly don't know about sarcasm?"

Golly, Clementine really tried to think. She had one idea, but it was perhaps not appropriate to mention it in mixed company. "Is it...*sexy*?" She cast a quick worried glance at Mr. Tremblay.

The manager of the Spruce Telephone Company doubled in two with laughter, and literally just slid out of his chair and on to the floor, trying to suck wind between great bellows of laughter. His shirt came untucked, one button popped, and his glasses were askew on his face. Everyone else was crying from laughing so hard, and Clementine wondered if they'd each taken a little nip of prohibited beverage before work.

Gauging by the response, Clementine asked, "It's dirty, isn't it, this sarcasm? Worse than sexy."

Hazel was the first to right herself, and she said, "Come, dear, and we'll look it up in the dictionary. Ladies, it's time to serve the public!" She seemed to have an extra pep in her step that morning as she herded all the operators upstairs. The workday had officially begun.

"You should have seen it, though," Florence rehearsed to Morgana and Isabelle. "When Clementine came leading the would-be robbers across the park to the sheriff, I never saw anything so funny in all my life! Matt and I were fit to die."

"Matt?" Helen asked.

"Clementine's brother. He's a looker!"

Matthew had never been called Matt, but since Florence was the boss, who was Clementine to correct her? She couldn't help smiling, though. Perhaps one or two of her brothers would soon be engaged, but things looked lonesome for Hardy, herself, and poor li'l Pete.

"What about Joe?" Vivian asked.

Florence replied, "Who? Joe who?"

The ladies shared smiles. It was time Florence moved on to greener pastures!

Once Clementine was seated, Hazel opened the dictionary.

> **Sarcasm,** *noun.*
>
> *The use of irony to mock or convey contempt.*

Clementine looked up at Hazel. "Well, that's not dirty

at all!" The ladies chuckled before they began patching calls in earnest.

The board lit up. Clementine answered, "Operator. How may I connect your call?"

"Hey, doll. Can I take you dancing tonight?"

"No, Mr. Pendleton. I've actually scheduled a well-deserved headache for tonight."

"You cruel thing," the reporter said.

"That's *sarcasm*."

"Too much weekend in your weekend, eh, doll? Well, it was worth a try. Did you catch the paper?"

"Yes."

"I tried my hardest to prove the fact that you're a real headliner."

"Only until a new headliner comes along."

"You're piercing my heart with these fickle accusations."

Helen, who was looming large, glared at Clementine until she ducked her head and disconnected the call. The board lit again. "Operator. How may I direct your call?"

"Jason Tremblay, please," a smooth-sounding voice requested.

Clementine wished she could see who she was talking to, but that would be impossible. "Just one second," she said, connecting the call and smiling when she heard the phone ring downstairs. The mind-boggling technology of telephones would never cease to amaze her.

When Clementine slipped to the breakroom for lunch, she was surprised to see a large bouquet of flowers for her. *Thank you for saving the day*. It was signed by Mr.

and Mrs. Hal Hoskins of the First Bank of Anchorage.

"Dear Mr. and Mrs. Curmudgeon, you're welcome," she whispered to the card.

Clementine nibbled on a piece of Mrs. Lawrence's leftover fried chicken and sloshed it all down with a cold glass of milk, gratis Contessa. Clementine really hadn't scheduled a headache, but to show her penitence to the Lawrences, she'd already determined to help with dishes and chores.

Mrs. Tremblay brought in a stack of newspapers. "I was instructed to get you several souvenir copies," she said.

"Thank Mr. Tremblay for me," Clementine replied, wondering who to give them to besides her four brothers. Julie hesitated momentarily, like she wanted to say something more, but then she shook her head and excused herself.

Saylor stopped by while Clementine was still at lunch. "Everyone is talking about you. And because you are my walking billboard, I've sold *seven* fringed flapper dresses just this very morning!"

"Really?" Clementine asked. "Thank you for coordinatin' me the first time and every time thereafter. And thanks even more for believin' I was somebody."

Saylor smiled, eyes twinkling. She was the kindest and pleasantest person of Clementine's acquaintances. "You're not just anybody, Clementine. You are my best friend in Anchorage, and Roxy is my best friend in Homer."

The fact that Saylor Ashton used "best" and "friend" in the same sentence—a sentence that was directly aimed at Clementine—well, it brought tears to her eyes. "Same. You are my best friend in Anchorage, and Roxy is my best friend in Homer also."

Saylor smiled again. "I came to invite you to have dinner with Andy and me."

"I," Clementine corrected.

"No, in this case, it's *me*," Saylor said with a giggle.

"I'll never understand the mother tongue." Clementine sighed, pretending to wave a white flag. "When?"

"Friday."

"I'm supposed to work the late shift."

"Raspberries," Saylor said, physically brushing the detail to the side. "That's all been taken care of."

"You really are magic, ain't ya?" How Saylor commanded so much respect from Mr. Tremblay was beyond Clementine's understanding. It was even harder to figure than the English language. Saylor had only worked at the Spruce Telephone Company six days—six!

"See ya then. By the way, you look very nice today. Classy."

Clementine wore her gray dress with a yellow cardigan, her dove gray shoes, and a gray, white, and yellow scarf. It was one of the first ensembles she'd tried on the day she met Saylor. "Thanks!"

"Oh, by the way, give one to Florence, would you?" She passed her an invitation to come and shop the new bridal collection at Asthon's Women's Shop.

"I don't know if things are all that serious with my Matthew," Clementine began. "The fellas have been in the woods awhile."

"It wouldn't hurt to plant it in their minds. Most women

know the art of subtle manipulation to use on a man."

"Okay, but I feel like maybe this is undermining Mr. Tremblay's mission here."

"I assure you, Clementine, all is fair in love and war. Oh, and by the way, Andy will call for you at quarter to six."

Clementine quietly set the table before Mrs. Lawrence even realized it. Then she went outside and tended the chickens and gathered the eggs for morning. It was close to milking time, so she took the bucket off the hook and went out to the barn. Contessa was happy to see her coming. She fed and milked the cow and poured warm milk into a dish for McTavish, the barn cat. The cat purred loudly. Clementine stroked his back for a second or two, saying, "Good kitty. Such a good kitty, Mr. McTavish."

She carried the milk bucket into the kitchen, surprising Ethel. The woman was a tad embarrassed about Guy's unkind words at the park. "Clementine, I'm sorry," she said at the exact moment Clementine said, "Mrs. Lawrence, I'm sorry."

Mrs. Lawrence took Clementine by the shoulders. "I tasted your pies. You deserved to win all three categories. I mean—the fruit one was close, but I too would have declared you the winner."

"That is very kind of you, Mrs. Lawrence. I promise I never stole your recipes or whatever it was Mr. Lawrence thought I did."

"I know it. He suspected you used chicanery."

"I didn't," Clementine declared stubbornly. "I promise, I used butter and flour like everyone else!"

Clementine didn't realize Mr. Lawrence had come into

the kitchen until she heard him laughing. It startled Clementine, and she whirled around. Why was he chuckling so hard? Had the whole town gone crazy? Then Mrs. Lawrence joined in—and the entire kitchen became a nuthatch.

"What's so funny?" she asked.

"You didn't use chicanery. You used butter," Mr. Lawrence cried.

"Well, I did. And I'm sorry, but old Floss and Blossom give the sweetest cream, which makes the bestest butter. I like your cow and everything, but—"

Mr. Lawrence drew wind enough to halt Clementine's ardent explanations. "Just please accept my apology. I realize you are far too innocent to have used *anything* but butter."

After the supper dishes were dried and put away, Clementine stepped onto the porch to get a breath of fresh air. She was surprised to see Matthew sitting in the swing with Florence.

"Hello Matthew," Clementine said.

"Hello Sis," he replied. And then, right in front of Clementine, Florence reached over and held Matthew's hand! He blushed in the porch light, but Florence just flashed him a big old smile and said, "Oh Matt, I love a man with a wagon."

"Saylor said most women know the art of subtle manipulation, but I'm not sure that's *subtle*," Clementine mused. "Well, have a nice evenin' you two. Drive home careful, Matthew—er *Matt*.

Then Clementine said goodnight to Matthew. As she

climbed the stairs to go to bed, she said, "There once was a couple of brothers, who suddenly were loved by others, and they couldn't but smile at these ladies of style, so I hope marriage is part of their druthers."

CHAPTER TWELVE

"A lady's imagination is very rapid; it jumps from admiration to love, love to matrimony in a moment."

Jane Austen

On Wednesday evening, as everyone was sitting down to dinner, there was a knock on the door. Tracy went to answer it and came back saying, "Clementine, the sheriff is here to see you."

Some of the ladies made "Ooh-la-la" comments, but Clementine was very angry at that overgrown oaf, and certainly not in the mood for romantic chiding. She cast a look of sarcasm to the ladies and left the dining room reluctantly.

Roy Martin stood with an apologetic stance, hat in his hand. "May I speak with you?"

"Am I to just listen, then?"

The sheriff's eyes rolled sideways, not understanding the question.

Clementine proceeded, "You never listen when I speak, so I take it I'm just to listen."

"Well, for that I am sorry, and I've come to apologize. You tried warning me about the bank."

Clementine now gave him the look of sarcasm, or what she deemed sarcasm to look like. "Go on," she said, still refusing to talk much.

"But I was so humiliated when you came dragging those men across the park."

"And not once did you thank me, or say a word, but to *The Anchorage Times*, you said plenty."

"That was all off the record! That pesky reporter has designs on you, so I feel as though he misreported my comments to cause a rift between us."

"Hank Pendleton can't kindle his own romance, no less ruin another! Honestly, Sherrif, there was no *us* to begin with." Clementine snatched Monday's paper off a little entry table and read, "'Sheriff Roy Martin said the actions taken by Clementine Clark and two of her brothers were foolish, beyond reckless, and might have ended terribly. The proper authorities should always be alerted first.' Is that what you said?"

"Yes, but—don't you see what danger you exposed yourself to?"

"I alerted you at least four times, and again as we danced at the park. You think I'm too purty and countrified-simple to have a brain in my head! And I might be dumb about a lot of things, but who was smarter in this situation? I tell you, I was, and I plan on runnin' for your job when your term is up."

The man paled considerably and stammered, "Women aren't sheriff material."

"Now you sound like Deputy Larry Whoever-he-is. I wasn't supposed to beat you good old boys at shootin', neither. I plan on beatin' you at a lot of things, so you'd better climb back in your truck and go warn 'em all."

"Well, I was hoping to apologize the way any gentleman should, but with such vulgar, immodest ambitions, perhaps you are not lady enough to receive it."

"I'm a modern—*and* a lady, but I ain't *your lady*, or *little lady*, or *purty lady*. I'm Clementine Clark! And you needn't come buzzin' around here any further." She grabbed the hat out of his hands and mashed it back onto his head. "But I will apologize as well. I used you for a taxi." She pivoted on her heel and went back into supper.

"The sheriff's gone now, and if there's any trouble—if any of you need the law—just let me know and I'll take care of it for you." She smiled convincingly, and the Switchboard Sisterhood cheered.

"I must admit," Mrs. Lawrence said, "we heard every word."

"Oh, well, now you know my intentions. I'm running for sheriff unless I become previously engaged."

"Which would you rather be?" Vivian asked, trying hard to understand such a walking contradiction of a gal. Like the others, she saw Clementine as both dumb and smart, but she was brave! And she was determined. Roxy would have said Clementine was a bundle of action verbs.

"As long as I'm engaged to a decent, respectful, and kind individual who doesn't talk down to me or treat me like a puppy, I'd rather be a wife and mother and do all the things for my own family that I liked to do for my brothers. But I ain't above pinning a star on my chest and arrestin' rascals, either. I ain't above shootin' the beer out of a gangster's hand."

Grandpa Jethro grinned at the spunky blonde. "You've got my vote, but I never was one of them good ol' boys."

Friday came, and Clementine had no job to go to. She spent the morning lazily reading on the porch swing. The autumn sunshine wasn't as warm as it looked, so she snuggled inside a quilt. The air was full of apples and cinnamon. Clementine loved the way seasons smelled and felt. She felt like kicking dried, fallen leaves around the yard, and so she did just to hear them crunch. She found a rake behind the chicken coop, and soon she had raked large piles. She remembered her pa throwing her into leaf piles when she was a girl.

She suddenly felt homesick. She went inside and asked, "Mrs. Lawrence, would it be all right if I used the kitchen to bake something to take to a dinner party I've been invited to?"

"Yes, most welcome! I have business downtown today and shouldn't be back until four."

Clementine had asked Matthew, to bring some fresh cream and butter out of the icehouse when he'd come to take a stroll around the lawn with Florence, so she set to work baking pies. She made a spicy apple pie because she knew it was Andy's favorite. Then she whipped up a brown sugar custard pie because Mrs. Kennedy said she was more addicted to it than a junkie to opium. Clementine giggled at the comment as the events from Saturday's Fall Festival still swirled around in her head.

She baked two pies of each so Mrs. Lawrence would have enough dessert to feed the ladies for supper, and that would repay her nicely for any pantry items that Clementine used.

While the pies baked, she ran upstairs to decide what to wear. The flapper fringe seemed too sexy, and her work ensembles not dressy enough. She settled on the pretty outfit she'd worn to Roxy and Reese's wedding. The dress that Hazel had taught her to dance in. The dress that made her decide she couldn't possibly be as loyal to the Spruce Telephone Company as she'd originally determined to be. Yes, that was what she'd wear.

She wrote in her journal the events of the week, finishing with a limerick. Her diaries and journals were full of them. *There once was a beautiful dress worn by a perfect mess—but to be fair, that dress didn't care, and a woman emerged, more or less.*

The pies cooled in the windowsill, and their pleasant aromas wafted all the way up to the third floor where Grandpa Jethro was fixing a leak. He came downstairs to see the pies. "For me?" he asked.

"Two will go to a dinner I've been invited to, and two shall stay here for Ethel to serve for supper."

"I'm half a mind to gobble one up and tell her there was only one to begin with."

"And which would you gobble?"

"I'd start with the apple. The way to a man's heart is through his piehole."

"Oh, really?" Clementine laughed. "I hadn't heard."

"If you are fixin' to feed this to a man tonight, you'll never be sheriff, and I was all set to vote."

"Well, it's just the Ashtons and me, so there's no worry, but the idea of being invited to a dinner party is so wonderful, especially by a celebrity like Saylor. It seemed ungraceful not to take somethin'."

"Oh, that saucy, scheming' little scudder's got somethin' up her sleeve," Jethro said, settling for a lump of brown sugar.

"Saylor?"

"That be the very one."

"Well, she *is* Emma Woodhouse," Clementine said, completely confuzzling the old man. "Except Saylor gets everything just right."

"That gal is a scallywaggin' thief!"

"Oh, please, Jethro, she was hungry and wanted a cookie. That is not any worse of a crime than your desire to make off with one *whole* pie and then lie about it."

The man angled his head thoughtfully, then said, "Well, if you're going to make a scallywag out of me, I'd better get back to work!"

Andy Ashton arrived at quarter to six, just as Saylor had instructed him to do. He was a gentleman in every way and opened the door for her, helping her put the pies in the back seat. "Please tell me these are coming with us," he said happily.

"I forgot to ask Saylor what I should bring, so I decided pie would be good."

"Award-winning pie," Andy said, lifting the apple one up to his nose. "What could be better?"

"That one's just for you, as Saylor's mentioned apple is your favorite fruit pie. I didn't have any pecans, which, if I remember correctly, is your first pick."

Andy put himself in the car and then he backed on to the street, chuckling.

"Yes?" Clementine asked, figuring she missed a joke.

"I was just thinking it wasn't that long ago that you rode in the rumble seat, leading your mule. And here you are today, one-hundred-and-seventy-five times more refined, but still feisty enough to shoot money bags out of the hands of robbers."

Clementine laughed with him, seeing how far she'd come, but also recognizing she was just the same on the inside. "It's awfully kind of you two to invite me to dinner," she said.

"You must reserve that comment until after you've tasted the food," Andy offered humorously.

"I'm certain Saylor can cook," Clementine said.

"She's been stewing around about it all week. She's desperate to impress you."

"Saylor, desperate? Mr. Ashton, I cannot believe it!"

"Flibbertigibbets like my wife live in the extremes, Miss Clark. She is usually buoyant, full of whimsy, flitting around, dusting the cobwebs off the sky, and lending stars her twinkle." Mr. Ashton drove with one hand and let the other talk. "But just as suddenly, Saylor can be thrust into the throws of agony, and all over some trifling detail like static cling or one misbehaving curl."

Clementine's brows arched higher and higher, never knowing Saylor to have any flaws. "We are all human," she ventured, not knowing what more to say.

"Me especially," Mr. Ashton agreed. "I'm more human than not, but oh, how I love my flibbertigibbet, and I do believe she's wild about me."

Mr. Ashton parked his car, and said, "Stay put so I can help you out." He ran around to the other side and opened the door. "I don't want anything happening to these," he said, reaching for the pies. Clementine laughed because he then said, "Oh, no! Now, will *you* be a gentleman and get the door?"

"I am a gentleman's gentleman," Clementine teased. She followed him up the stairs and into the apartment.

Saylor was dressed impeccably in a belted rust dress. The drop-waist skirt was pleated so smartly. She wore beige beads and earbobs, and two-tone rust and beige oxfords.

She was sophisticated! "You are the most stylish person in the whole wide world," Clementine said.

"Look at you! So perfect in your blue—I was actually hoping you'd wear this! I love it on you."

"But you're dressed for the season, and you make me think of cinnamon, and caramel, and stewed apples with steep peaks of whipped cream."

"I thank you," Saylor said with a wink. "Those pies look divine. I had a sneaking suspicion you'd bring one, but I never bargained on two."

The trio walked into the kitchen. A man wearing an apron was transferring pot roast onto a serving platter. Trust Saylor to hire a chef! "Mmm, smells delish," Clementine said. That was the universal compliment to give when being catered to. Helen had taught her socially polite gestures and comments while at Roxy's wedding.

"Just a moment," the cook said. He smiled and walked into the guest bedroom. When he returned, he sported a suit jacket and tie, and gone was the apron. He held a chair out for Clementine, and she said, "How kind," and sat, feeling some odd way about him. It was sneaky of Saylor not to warn her the handsome chef was staying for dinner.

"This is Clementine Clark," Saylor said as Andy politely held her chair. Both gentlemen sat at the same time.

"I recognized her from the paper," the man said.

The utter reality of her past week settled in on Clementine until her cheeks turned the color of measles, at the very least, and possibly scarlet fever. Saylor was the type of celebrity people would say that about. "Hi, I recognized your face from your picture in the paper," and that sort of thing—but not Clementine!

"Oh," Clementine stammered. The man smiled, revealing one deep-set dimple. "I like your smile—that dimple," she admitted honestly. "It's so vogue not to sport a matched set."

Andy's brows rose to the occasion while the other man's one dimple deepened. Clementine felt the need to follow that with something, but it was bound to be worse.

"Did you read that somewhere?" Saylor asked, beating her to the punch.

"I must have," Clementine said, grateful for a best friend in Anchorage. And at the dinner table.

"I am happy to meet you, Miss Clark." He reached across the table to shake her hand. "I must admit I was eager to meet you! I am—"

"Oh, this is my uncle, Otto Lloyd," Saylor said.

"Nice to meet you," Clementine said, still pumping his hand up and down. "I'm Clementine Clark."

"Yes." Andy chuckled. "We've already established *your* identity."

For the love of Pete! And Matthew, Heath, and Hardy. Clementine wished someone would just stitch her mouth shut. "Oh—I apologize," she said, shaking her head quickly as if to resettle things in her head. Did this beautiful and handsome stranger just say he was *eager* to meet her?

Mr. Lloyd just smiled, that glorious smile with only one dimple. "No need."

"Your name sounds familiar," Clementine said, wishing she ever knew the best things to say.

"Uncle Otto is your employer," Saylor prodded pleasantly.

Suddenly the lines connected! This was the true owner of the Spruce Telephone Company. "You are a good deal younger than I pegged you to be," Clementine confessed, eyes suddenly searching his hand for a wedding ring. Her smile brightened instantly at not seeing one.

"I came to Anchorage to thank you for saving our accounts. You have done a stellar job in both representing and protecting my interests here. I trust the Tremblays purchased a stack of newspapers for you as I instructed them to. It's not every day such a capable employee makes the headlines!"

So, the complimentary newspapers were from *him*—and perhaps it was he, and not Saylor, who had cleared her work schedule. "I can't believe an important man such as yourself cooked our supper," Clementine said, nearly worshipping the pot roast on the platter.

"I enjoy cooking," Mr. Lloyd said.

"I do too," Clementine cried, finding it miraculous that they had *so* much in common—chiefly, both knowing Saylor, and both liking to cook.

"Yes, I read that your pies swept the competition last Saturday as well. My mouth watered just reading about them."

"I baked a couple of pies and brung 'em to dinner," Clementine confessed eagerly, possibly upsetting the notion that she was an heiress or something.

"'Brought' them," Saylor corrected.

"Yes, I baked 'em, I brung 'em, and I *brought* them."

Andy and Saylor exchanged wary glances, but Otto seemed all the more intrigued. "Pie, you say? Then what are we doing wasting time with this infernal pot roast?"

"It's not infernal because once you eat it, it'll be internal," Clementine joked. She speared a morsel of it with her fork and popped it smack in her mouth. Once it was chewed and swallowed, she followed with, "That could win an award of its own, Mr. Lloyd." Then Clementine let her eyes sparkle in his direction. Hopefully, the kitchen lighting was bright enough to telegraph the full effect.

CHAPTER THIRTEEN

*"Food is not simply organic fuel to keep your body
and soul together, it is a perishable art that must be
savoured at the peak of perfection."*

E.A. Bucchianeri

What do you call this pie?" Mr. Lloyd asked, raising his fork to inspect a slice of the old-fashioned brown sugar custard pie.

"I call that matrimony pie," Clementine lied smack through her teeth, "because once you taste it, you're goin' to want to marry me."

Andy choked on his own slice of spicy apple while Saylor cast her eyes toward her debonair bachelor uncle, to gauge his response, but it was somewhat different than what she expected. Otto's fork was frozen in midair. He was suddenly not looking at the pie, but overlooking it, content to study Clementine. She was a walking contradiction of everything, and all at once, too.

Saylor's eyes shifted toward Clementine. She was a bundle of nerves, caught between not knowing what to say and saying too much, but she embodied innocent childlike sincerity, even if she did just fabricate a new name for her old pie. Clementine's eyes sparkled and her cheeks pinked, for she'd crawled out on a most uncomfortable limb with her bold dishonesty.

Saylor looked at her uncle again. He smiled slowly,

then lifted the pie to his lips to judge for himself. His lips parted and his eyes closed, an action that drew Clementine forward in her chair. She was eager to see the look of pleasure cross his features, and she didn't have to wait long.

Andy nudged Saylor's foot with his own, silently motioning toward Clementine's hand. Before the woman even knew what she was doing, she had clasped Mr. Lloyd's left hand across the table, as if waiting in anticipation. Saylor's eyes bugged, and she shot another frantic look at Andy, but he smiled as if to say, *"You acted on your hunch, Seattle Sue, and it paid off."*

Otto Lloyd didn't open his eyes for a whole minute. He squeezed Clementine's hand, though, letting her know his mouth was fully engaged, but to her or the pie, was the question. When he did open his eyes, he said, "Mmm! Matrimony pie, huh? The first bite was worth at least six months of courting you."

Clementine utterly beamed. "By the time you finish that slice, then, we're apt to have three or four kids runnin' around!"

Saylor giggled and Andy horn blasted, which wasn't proper dinner etiquette. Clementine said, "Golly, your behavior at the dinner table is as bad, if not worse, of a crime as me saying, 'I brung two pies.'"

Mr. Lloyd smiled wide, unable to conceal his amusement. Clementine was the most unique and incredibly quirky gal he'd ever been introduced to. "Well, let's see." He took a second bite, and like the first, his eyes closed, and a look of absolute pleasure rolled across his face. Even his shoulders relaxed, and a small moan escaped his throat.

"See that?" Clementine quizzed Andy. "That's honeymoon level right there. I can't wait to find out where we went."

Oh, now the horn blasting was worse. The Ashtons laughed uncontrollably, and only Mr. Lloyd remained at a nearly stoned degree of decorum. Clementine continued to clutch his hand for support. Somehow believing Mr. Lloyd couldn't hear them while under the effects of a honeymoon, Clementine whispered, "Grandpa Jethro said the way to a man's heart is through his piehole. That's why I didn't bake a cake."

Laughter, *drunken* laughter without a drop of demon liquor, exploded around the table. Even the well-mannered gentleman from Seattle couldn't hold it back, though it nearly caused him to choke. Clementine, being a good sport, joined in the ruckus, and finally, when Otto Lloyd was able to draw wind, he winked at her and said, "Madam, I have most effectively been seduced."

Clementine gazed appreciatively. She willed the sunset from the horizon to radiate through her eyes, her smile, and her soul. Otto Lloyd had already signed his name in her heart.

All four tied aprons around themselves as they cleaned up the dishes. "We thought we should go dancing," Saylor said. "This will get us there sooner!"

"Where?" Clementine asked.

"The *North Wind Natasha*," Saylor said. "It's where Andy and I tied the knot."

"Oh, the famous speakeasy with sails," Clementine gasped, thinking this sounded like a big adventure. "Good thing I recently learned how to dance on the ferry. I'm tellin' ya, those waves can be tricky. If I start dancin' sideways, you'll know it's the water's fault."

Otto Lloyd pinched his lips together. It wouldn't be kind to laugh at the girl every second, but she was a refreshing change from the high-society bores he typically met. They were the reason he'd never married. He hated piety and pomp! It was a dishonest game, looking for love among the leisure class, and like *Gatsby*, their morals usually proved the lowest class of all.

"What if I go sideways first?" he asked.

"I'll join ya, Mr. Lloyd, and then you'll have at least one friend down there with ya."

This time Andy smiled. His darling Saylor had been right, of course. Clementine Clark *was* the perfect antidote for all that troubled her jaded uncle.

Clementine covered the pies with a towel. "Now, Andy, that apple pie is for you, but you should share some with Saylor. And Mr. Lloyd, the matrimony pie is all yours."

"That is very kind," he said.

"Mr. Lawrence—who owns the boardinghouse where I stay—well, he accused me of using chicanery to win the contest last Saturday. And anyway, I balled up my fists, and I said, 'I did not! I used butter and flour like everyone else.' And then he apologized."

Mr. Lloyd couldn't keep the laughter away that time, and he reacted strangely. He pulled Clementine toward him and kissed her forehead. "Sorry," he said, astonished at his own behavior, "but I've never met anybody as good as you are before."

Clementine's eyes were wide. That poor man! He must have had a very sad life. "I don't mind. In fact, if it makes ya feel better, you're welcome to aim just a few inches lower so I could kiss ya back."

Saylor looked at Andy, and her mouth shaped into a surprised, albeit happy, little O, as in, "Oh, this has gone better than even *I* could have expected." Then she smiled like the cat that was in the cream. If her millionaire uncle married her first attempt at coordinating and introducing a person into society, Saylor would consider herself a professional match-making stylist.

The ride to the *North Wind Natasha* was a pleasant one. Andy parked near the docks, and Mr. Lloyd was quick to scurry around and open Clementine's door just as Andy opened Saylor's. "By the way," he said in a low voice, "I forgot to mention how much I love your dress, and your hat—"

"And my shoes," Clementine prodded, pointing down at her feet proudly. "Your niece—she coordinated me."

"Yes, and your shoes," Otto chuckled. "And I appreciate that you haven't bobbed your hair like so many of the ladies do nowadays."

"Pa always said my hair waved in the wind like a golden flag. If I whacked it, it would only wave like a small circus pennant. So, I ain't never cut it, and I also ain't never been to the circus, but I've read about it." Suddenly Clementine stopped talking. "I'm sorry. I meant to use better grammar! Let me try again." She cleared her throat and said, "I *have never* been to the circus."

Mr. Lloyd received the apology warmly. He held out his arm for Clementine as they followed the Ashtons across the street and up the gangplank. "Here's a little secret," he said. "I ain't never enjoyed myself more than I am enjoying myself with you."

"Must be the pie," Clementine faltered. Her cheeks flushed and her knees grew somewhat weak. "Whoa," she said, stumbling a bit. Mr. Lloyd slowed his steps, helping her steady herself. "Oh, thank you, Mr. Lloyd. I couldn't best Pete in an Indian leg wrestle tonight, that's for sure."

"Pete?"

"He's my youngest older brother."

"I haven't Indian leg wrestled anyone in years," Mr. Lloyd admitted.

"If ya get itchin' to, I'll happily oblige you a match. But not in my best dress."

"Of course." Otto nodded. He looked ahead and called, "I've got it," as Andy and Saylor approached a deckhand taking money. He drew a couple of bills from his wallet.

"Thanks, Uncle," Saylor said.

"Where were you on our first date?" Andy asked comically, even though the cover charge was only a dollar per couple. Saylor turned around and flashed a quick wink at Clementine. Things seemed to be going well for her countrified best friend in Anchorage.

Once Mr. Lloyd put his wallet away, he took Clementine by the hand, which was a much more intimate gesture than just lending an arm. Clementine sighed dreamily.

"Everything all right, Miss Clark?"

"Yes. I was just thinkin' how bad I'd be at arm wrestlin' right now, too."

"I see," Mr. Lloyd said, not seeing at all, but he didn't care! She was lovely, and fresh, and original enough to pique his interest for at least fifty years. "I won't place any bets on you, then."

Clementine's eyes were large as they walked past

dinner tables with all kinds of consumers drinking beer, whiskey, ales, and wine. "If I was sheriff, I'd arrest them all," she said.

"Oh, I take it you are a law-abiding citizen?"

"I try," Clementine said.

"No champagne for you, then?"

"Is it strictly prohibited in the great Territory of Alaska?"

"I'm afraid so," Otto answered.

"Then no."

"A teetotaler! I like a woman who's strong in her convictions."

"What about you, Mr. Lloyd?"

"On occasion I have been known to take a sip."

"When I'm sheriff, I'll arrest ya."

"When you are sheriff, I shall gladly surrender."

Just then Clementine noticed Hazel, dancing with friends. Hazel saw her in the same instant, but rushed right past her, saying, "Mr. Lloyd, what an honor to have you in town! Might we expect you at the office tomorrow?"

"Probably not tomorrow, Miss Gagnon." They shook hands. Hazel nodded at the others, then went back to her group.

"Which one is that?" Mr. Lloyd asked.

"Hazel," Clementine whispered near his ear.

"I can't tell them apart."

Clementine giggled. "Well, that's Hazel. She's a funner sort than Helen, who is probably home dancing with her book."

Just then Clementine noticed Heath angling towards the group of ladies. "There's my brother!"

"Your brother?" Otto asked.

"Yes."

"You'd better introduce us," Otto said.

"Proud to, sir." She dragged him by the arm. "Heath, this is Mr. Otto Lloyd. He's my bosses' boss and Saylor's uncle."

Heath eyed the man up and down. "That's Li'l Sis," he said, saying so much more than anybody could hear except for men who knew the code about sisters.

"I shall guard her as my own," Otto promised.

"That's my second-to-oldest brother by nine minutes," Clementine explained once the introductions were through.

"Nine minutes?"

"Yeah, Hardy beat him out of the chute."

"Might I ask how old they are?"

"Forty-two," Clementine said. "Add 'em up and they're eighty-four."

"That's also my age. Forty-two, that is."

"I always imagined Mr. Otto Lloyd to be older—like sixty-five, and with white hair. Instead, you're just so elegant-like with a touch of silver in your sideburns. You're the best type of forty-two."

"My father was once sixty-five, and he had white hair," he said. Otto studied Clementine's face while gathering her in his arms for a waltz. Hazel gave Clementine a thumbs-up as she twirled by.

Just then Heath asked Hazel to dance, and Otto asked Clementine if her brother was serious about the socializing redhead.

"It looks that way to me," Clementine said. "If she breaks his heart, I hope you will have Mr. Tremblay fire her! I shouldn't have favorites, but Heath *is* my favorite. He's the most like Pa."

"And what shall the punishment be if you break my heart, Miss Clark?"

"I would never break your heart," Clementine declared. "You, Mr. Lloyd, are precisely the gosh-dern *some kind of wonderful* that I've been waitin' for."

"If that is the case, then God bless your patience." He drew her hand to his lips tenderly, imparting a kiss so delicate, it was likely made out of glass.

"Ooh," Clementine gasped. "That gave me the flutters."

Clementine was sad for the dance to end, but the jazzy rhythms of the Charleston were fun, too. Saylor and Andy were the showstoppers, but Hazel and Heath, and Otto and Clementine, danced on either side of them, not needing to worry about being in the spotlight. The Black Bottom Rag was next, but Heath dragged himself to a table for supper.

"For a forty-two-year-old, you dance purty good," Clementine said to Otto.

"Do you mind me asking your age?"

"I'm twenty-six."

"Are you bothered by the disparity?" And he meant in age.

"No, and I don't have rheumatism, either."

Otto Lloyd laughed gleefully. "Neither do I," he said. "No rheumatism here."

"Health is a precious gift," Clementine remarked. "And I ain't never had no stye in my eye, neither."

"Such beautiful eyes," Otto said, "should have no styes!"

"Do you like poetry?" Clementine quizzed, as if she were a pushy reporter out for a stroll.

"It's all right. Do you?"

"Only if they're funny," Clementine said. "I make up extemparubious ones—limericks, mostly."

"Extemporaneous?" Otto asked, seeking clarification.

"That's the one! I knew it was ex-temp-a-somthin'. Yep, I make those up off the top of my head."

"Show me."

"There once was a silly ol' pie, and a handsome, incredible guy—who looked at this girl—" she thumped herself in the chest, "and made her toes curl, and her spirit soared up to the sky." She swept both arms upward to illustrate.

Otto Lloyd stopped moving right in the middle of the song. He took Clementine by the hand and led her to a cabin door and out onto a deck. Aside from ocean sounds, the deck was quiet, and it provided relief to the ears. "My darling Clementine," he said, lifting both hands to his lips. He kissed them tenderly, never taking his eyes off her face. "It's untoward of me to be so bold when we've only just met—"

"But I'm a modern," Clementine countered breathlessly. Then she leaned up on her tiptoes and kissed him smack on his handsome mouth.

That kiss was amazing, but by the third one, they'd perfected the recipe.

CHAPTER FOURTEEN

"Any man who can drive safely while kissing a pretty girl is simply not giving the kiss the attention it deserves."

Albert Einstein

Clementine was scheduled to work Saturday, but Jason Tremblay received a call from Otto Lloyd, telling him she'd not be in that day. Instead, Mr. Lloyd picked her up in a new car. As he climbed out, Florence cried, "Are you kidding me? You're going driving with *the* Mr. Otto Lloyd, owner of the Spruce Telephone Company?"

"Oh, do you know him?" Clementine asked.

All the ladies began squawking at once. "How is this possible?"

Tracy giggled. "You know he's loaded, don't you?"

"He's as high society as they come," Vivian finished, and Nora just shook her head in disbelief.

"But he's down to earth, and he makes a great pot roast," Clementine said, "and I've kissed him proper, smack on that mouth, and I plan on kissing him some more if he'll let me."

The ladies funneled through the porch door, across the lawn, and through the gate, acting nearly starstruck that a man of his station should come to the Lawrence Boarding House. "Hello, Mr. Lloyd," Florence called.

"Good morning. I have something for you ladies." He passed an envelope to each one. Inside were crisp ten-dollar bills.

"Why, thank you," several cried upon seeing the bonus. "Thank you so much!"

"I appreciate you all for representing my company so well. Florence, would you mind giving these to the Tremblays and Gagnon twins when you get to work?"

"I'd be happy to," she said, feeling singled out in a special way. Several of the women cast backward glances over their shoulders, scarcely believing the millionaire could fall for...Clementine Clark. But there it was on full display. Mr. Lloyd opened his arms, and Clementine stepped right in.

"Oh," Nora gasped. "The embrace is nearly as beautiful as the automobile."

"That's a Model J," Ruby said, and she would have known, being the daughter of wealthy parents and interested in Hollywood. "I didn't even know they sold cars like that in Anchorage!"

"They only had *one*," Florence said, "Matt and I drove by Alaska Auto Sales on the wagon, and he said he bet that curmudgeon, Hal Hoskins, ordered it in special just so he could show off."

The ladies and their comments soon drifted out of earshot. Clementine said, "Otto, that really is a pretty car!" She ran her hand along the sleek white exterior. "And I'm so glad it's yours. I don't much care for those curmudgeons, even if they did send me flowers."

Mr. Lloyd laughed. "What is your definition of a curmudgeon?"

"I never heard the word in my life until I began working.

Helen and Hazel are especially against anyone with money being cranky with people who don't."

"I see how that would merit such a title, then."

"Oh, but they ain't against you! You're *revered* around that place."

"Well, I thought we'd go driving and have a picnic. Do you have a jacket in case it gets cold?"

"I forgot to grab it—I'll be right back." She darted across the yard and into the house. Clementine pinched herself as she clipped up the stairs. Yesterday she was lazing on the front porch swing, reading a romance novel, and today—she was *in* one!

She checked her reflection in the glass once more. She wore her fun plaid dress with red shoes and matching cloche. She sighed once, wishing for Saylor's wardrobe, perhaps, but this would have to do. She certainly couldn't wear what she wore the previous night, and the sexy dress wouldn't do for a daytime picnic.

She dashed back down the stairs, calling, "Have a great day," to Jethro and Mrs. Lawrence.

"She's late for work," she heard Mrs. Lawrence say with a cluck of disapproval.

Otto leaned against the shiny chrome bumper. He smiled at Clementine as she ran, pell-mell, wild and free, toward him. There was no proper "walking like a lady" with this one. Not only didn't she live by the rules, but she never knew half of them to begin with.

"I'm so glad you waited for me," she squealed as she got closer.

Otto laughed, feeling youthful exuberance. "You are the sole purpose as to why I'm here—where would I have gone without you?"

"I don't know," she countered with a face full of sunshine. "But I've been excited all night to see you this morning. And here it is, morning, and I'm nearly too excited to keep up with it!"

"Thank you for your honesty, and for not putting on airs. Clementine, I adore everything about you." He helped her inside the luxurious vehicle. "You make this car look good," he said.

"Like it needs any help from me," Clementine bantered. "These seats are genuine leather, and oh, it smells good in here." She closed her eyes and took a deep whiff.

"I come from a family of automotive connoisseurs. Grandfather Avondaire was crazy about them, and Uncle Eldon is out to collect the best."

"Kind of like my family is about saws."

"Saws? Tell me more."

"Pa built a mill on Ship Creek, out of town about four miles. Used to be out of town by six miles, but things are growin' and Hardy says that's called progress. It's not a big operation, but sufficient enough, and I'll tell you, a lot of this town has been built with Earl Clark & Sons lumber. But Pa and my brothers knew all the best saws to use, and for which types of timber."

"I confess to being entirely stupid on the subject."

"If ya want, I could show ya."

"Okay, Miss Clark, lead the way."

"The road ain't paved the whole way."

"Cars aren't made of paper—they can be washed, and we'll wash this one."

Otto Lloyd was as kind a man as his niece was nice. He never looked down his nose at the log cabin the Clarks lived in. In fact, he complimented the structure as well-built. He followed Clementine around as she introduced him to Hilde the mule, and then to ol' Floss and Blossom, the cows. "And these are my hens," she said, lifting one. "This here is Edwina, and that brown hen, scratchin' yonder, is Millicent."

"Have you named all of them?" Otto asked.

"Well, there's Henrietta and Phyllis over by the barn door. I've got a Geraldine and a Jemima around here someplace, but I can't tell 'em from Eunice and Stella."

"You're something special," Otto said.

Clementine kissed the chicken on the top of her sweet chicken head, saying, "But none are so sweet as you, Edwina. Not even Irene."

Otto took the Edwina from Clementine's arms and placed her on the ground. "Pretend I am a chicken, please. Where would you kiss me?"

"Oh, right here in the barnyard, I reckon."

Otto shook his head. Then he pointed to his mouth, and Clementine gave him a giggly kiss.

Otto pulled away to study her. His expression was intense, as every emotion played across his face. "I love you, Clementine."

"I love you too," Clementine said, unable to keep tears from spilling down her cheeks. She leaned in for another kiss, and that kiss turned into five more, and soon enough, he'd swept her into his arms and ran with her to the creekbank where he'd spread a quilt. He unpacked the picnic basket, revealing sandwiches made from leftover roast beef.

"I swear I never had a better sandwich," Clementine said.

"I swear I've never had better company."

"I used to daydream up and down the creekbank about bringin' just the right fella here sometime. Thanks for bein' him."

"Thanks for being you," Otto said after sloshing his sandwich down with a thermos of coffee.

Clementine took another bite. "These really are good."

"I hope you like pickles," he said.

"I do."

"And mustard?"

"I do."

"And matrimony pie?" Otto gazed into Clementine's eyes, counting the stars in each one.

"I do," Clementine said with a shaky voice.

"Good, because I brought the rest of it to enjoy with you." Otto dished two slices onto small plates.

He took a bite and closed his eyes again, allowing himself to savor it. And when he opened his eyes, he rolled onto one knee. "Clementine Clark, will you marry me? I mean, since you've just said 'I do' three times and are well practiced?" He fished a ring box out of his pocket. He slid an immodest diamond right up her finger. "Marry me, oh, my darlin' Clementine. I love you madly!"

"I will! But after only four bites of matrimony pie? I love you the way Ma must've loved my pa. You do know I was gonna run for sheriff, though, don't ya?"

"If that is your dream, pursue it. Darling, I can live anywhere! If you want to live in Anchorage and run for sheriff, I shall make Anchorage my home, too."

"But even more than wanting that, I want to be your wife and have your babies."

Otto closed his eyes again, just savoring the rush of being so in love and hearing Clementine's hopeful desires. "Then that is what I want as well."

"But...Mr. Tremblay is going to be so disappointed in me!"

"Clementine, you silly gal, don't you realize he'll be working for you?"

Clementine laughed outright. "Golly, I can suspect things of *him* now!"

Otto chuckled and took another bite of the pie. "Yes, ma'am. And Saylor will become your niece."

Clementine gasped. "My favorite niece in Anchorage! Who'd have ever thunk it? I have put that gal on quite a pedestal."

"She wrote to me about you several weeks ago. She said something to the effect of, 'I think I may have found a pure-enough soul to match your own, dear uncle. Her name is Clementine, and there's no pretense in her at all. She's lived a humble, honest life, devoid of ulterior motives.'"

"That's not entirely true. I used Sheriff Martin as a personal taxi a few times."

"I forgive you," Otto said.

"Let's get married tomorrow," Clementine suggested. "Saylor and Andy got married in six days, but we should do it in just three."

"As you wish."

"Your mother won't be mad?"

"Clementine, I'm forty-two—I promise she'll dance a jig to learn I fell in love with one so *un-boring* as you!"

"Let's eat the rest of that pie and see what happens next."

"What happens next is…I teach you to drive that car I bought you."

"My car?"

"Well, of course it is!"

"Wait till the switchboard gals hear about this! I really don't need to be sheriff now. I just wanted to get elected so I'd have myself a free vehicle. I figured, if I was sheriff instead of him, I could just drive my own self places and not have to put up with him callin' me his 'little lady' all the time."

"You can drive to Ashton's and Saylor can knock herself out fitting you in the dress of your dreams, and you can shop for all the clothes and shoes you want."

"And delicate underthings?" Clementine squealed, unable to contain her excitement.

"Let's not break me into too much of a sweat, but yes—of course! Then you can drive all the packages to the home I bought last night when I couldn't sleep."

"We have a—a house?"

"I needed one in Anchorage anyway. Whenever I've visited in the past, I've had to stay at the hotel and I've never slept a wink. It was nicer staying with Saylor on this visit, but I figured maybe we'd like some privacy… and maybe some chickens."

"Privacy—and—chickens?" Clementine knocked Otto back on the blanket, peppering him with kisses.

"It's a lovely cottage next door to Andy's parents' home. There's a shady lot behind the house, and plenty of room for a garden, or flowers, fruit trees, a milk cow— whatever you want."

"Well, just how big of a shady lot is there?"

"Five acres."

"Jumpin' Jiminy!" Clementine cried. "I got me a house and five acres?"

"And a tributary of Campbell Creek cuts a pretty diagonal right through the northeast corner."

"Oh, Otto! How many happy tears are you gonna make me cry? I can't believe it."

"And we have a mansion in Seattle if you ever want to visit."

"Jeepers, a mansion? Saylor and Ruby both say Seattle is sensational! Otto, we could honeymoon there—and I could meet your mother."

"Absolutely, and she shall love you as I do. Clementine Clark, we're rich, you know, but we ain't cranky about it."

Clementine looked all around her. She could see the cabin, and the hens scratching in the barnyard. She could hear the creek rushing along, and smell sweet clover, and feel the autumn sunshine. "I've *always* been rich, dearest Otto, but I ain't never once been a curmudgeon."

EXCERPTS FROM CLEMENTINE'S JOURNAL

"Otto has given me the world, but I love home most of all. We shall never outgrow the cottage."

11/2/1925

Today I married my Otto dear, and honestly felt my mother near—oh, the joy that filled my lonesome heart, for heavenly thoughts she did impart, lettin' me know she has always been right here.

3/14/1926

I found a friend in Otto's mother, who raised him right, not like another! She, herself, is a league above, when it comes to sharin' love, but she's careful not to smother.

6/15/1927

Tiny daughter at my breast, I promise we shall love you best For all your days, in all the ways Your daddy and I will protect your nest.

9/4/1936

The position of sheriff, I wanted to run—to win would have been great fun but imagine my glee when I didn't. Tee-hee! But I'm still the best hand with a gun.

11/2/1945

There once was a happy-ever-after, and a cottage filled with glee and laughter. Babies came, one by one, two girls and then a tiny son—and love swelled right up to the rafters.

2/14/1956

There once was a grandma, Clementine, still in love with her Valentine. Grandpa Otto, so dear, is always right here treating our family most kind!

11/2/1964

I make the sweetest, yummiest butter from the cream of happy udder. I still bake with a reason, delicious pies in their season, that keeps Otto's heart all a'flutter.

10/26/1971

The Fall Festival has become tradition, every year a new rendition of award-winning pies, and shooting clouds from the skies. I've never lost one competition.

ABOUT THE AUTHOR

*"If there's a day when the world loses its humor, I
simply write a happier one into existence."*

June Marie Saxton

June Marie Saxton owns Bear Necessities of Montpelier, a nutritional clinic, bookstore, and children's boutique. June Marie enjoys interacting with her clients and customers, and truly loves the character traits she sees in others. "The people I meet, and learn to love, all seem to plant seeds in my mind from which more stories grow."

She and her husband, Mike, also own Saxton Ranch. "I love country living," Saxton claims, "and never see myself living anywhere else."

June Marie writes because it makes her happy. "I hope my love for it is evidence that I *should* continue painting with words, and not take up knitting or math." She has authored eighteen books.

Titles by June Marie include *Dancing with the Moon, Beckon, Into the Second Springtime, Pirate Moon, Emerald Fire, Ball Baby, Veil of Azure Sequins, Mach 16, Diamonds of the Quarter, Improper Son, Tolliver, Haley at the Hop, Perfectly Pepper, The Doctor of Devonshire, Rose of Ravenswood, Saylor, Roxy, and Clementine.* June Marie also helped get her dad's book, *Whirlwind on the Outlaw Trail,* published.

To stay abreast of Saxton's writing and releases, go

to www.junemariesaxton.com and sign up for her
newsletter.

Follow her on social media @ https://www.facebook.
com/junemariesaxton

Made in the USA
Monee, IL
16 October 2023